Reliable Light

✖ STORIES BY

Meredith Steinbach

RUTGERS UNIVERSITY PRESS

New Brunswick and London

The author wishes to express her gratitude to the Mary Ingraham
Bunting Institute of Radcliffe College, Harvard University; the National
Endowment for the Arts; and the Rhode Island State Council on the
Arts for their generous support.
Selections from this work have previously appeared, some in altered
form, in *Antioch Review, Massachusetts Review, Southwest Review, Tyuonyi,*
and *Five Fingers Review.*

Library of Congress Cataloging-in-Publication Data
Steinbach, Meredith
Reliable light / Meredith Steinbach.
p. cm.—(Rutgers Press fiction)
ISBN 0-8135-1531-9
I. Title.   II. Series.
PS3569.T37546R45   1990
89-29177
CIP
813'.54—dc20

British Cataloging-in-Publication information available

for my sister, Sandra

$\mathscr{C}ontents$

Reliable Light

$\mathcal{S}$parking

S H E had been with Monsieur a few times and found him silky, quiet, kind. He said he'd a brother, a father known for his paintings, and a mother dead—they did not talk about any of that. How Monsieur had come to live in a lowly hotel in the brown-gray gut of Chicago didn't seem to matter. It was not a squat little building with a mission sign in front of it but a hotel nearly fourteen stories high and peopled with interesting types.

On that first afternoon when he brought her home with him, he showed her the worn, red-carpeted hall: there was the door of the maker of matchstick churches six feet high with windows of comic strips translucent with melted wax, there lived a man whose company had gone poof on the Exchange overnight, there one who sold brushes for even the cleaning of the most inner ears, and there, that door had been broken down twice from the inside with an axe. Yes, he said quietly trying perhaps to heighten the moment ever so slightly, those tenants put on high heels together, dresses, and wigs. She smiled almost inattentively at him. It was comforting to know she had somewhere to go where real people lived, especially now that she had started her new job and knew no one, trusted no one, was frightened continually of new sights and sounds. Perhaps that was how she had come to be with Monsieur; everything was random now that it was new.

Her boss was an immensely ferocious lawyer with a handlebar mustache. He might have been on a circus poster lifting hundred pound bells at the end of a bar. She had seen the line of his shorts under his pin-striped pants and the big ruff of hair sticking out from the scooped bodice of his undershirt when he unfastened the top button of his shirt and threw down his tie at the center of his brown leather chair. If he had stripped down to his boxer shorts and tank top—yes, he would look almost a cartoon, but with heft, someone who might swallow an entire trout in a gulp if you held it over his head. All the clerks, even the ones who had been there the longest were afraid of him. He knew just how to find out your soft spots, they said.

Still it was the best situation she had ever had. She lived in an apartment that was comfortable and languid with light in an old stucco building surrounded by trees. Outside, on the front street a pair of squirrels nested in the carriage light, building it up with twigs, and not even City Maintenance would bother them. She had a little money to send to her mother who refused to move even now from the village where she had been born. For continued luck she wore a little tin necklace against her dark skin—to carry her through.

But at night, when the traffic on the side street outside her building had died down to an occasional buzz, she lay afraid in her bed and listened to the sound of her boss assailing her in front of the others as he had done casually and continually since he'd hired her three months before. And today the boss had taken up calling her, with a smile and a melody in his voice, by the names of various breeds of dogs. At first she had not recognized what it was he was saying in such a friendly tone; many of the words she had had to look up when she'd arrived at home, a burning in her face as she stared into the book. But she was a very fine clerk, even he, The Terror—as the other clerks called him, would not have said otherwise.

Now it happened again that she awakened this way, all in a

sweat with her nightgown soaked through and sticking to her breasts and belly, along both sides. In the light falling from the street her arms had gone slightly blue. Her heart leapt so hard against her ribs that a flutter had started up near the juncture of her shoulder and chest almost as if a bee had walked in and gone wild. Paralyzed, she lay in her bed before the early August heat that rolled off the avenue and in through her window. She bore the mounting worry that on the next day, frazzled, sleepless, and worn, she would make mistakes at work and he would have real cause for her degradation. She must have nodded off finally, she realized, for then, almost before she knew it, she was awake again, sitting upright in her bed in a daze.

Vividly, so vividly, she had dreamed that she'd stabbed him with a knife. Yes, the blade had sunk in directly between the great sacks of his lungs and split his sternum in half. There had been a certain relief in the dream as he lumbered forward and fell back with two white marbles staring out of his head. But then, soon after, the relief was curtailed: for there, in the dream, first the black rounded button and then the two floppy ears and the pink tongue of a yellow dog burst clean out of his chest. And then the spaniel cocked its head—patiently waiting as if for her excuse.

At the start of the following weekend, she made plans to go out with young Monsieur. Ah Saturday, and it seemed only a few hours from morning to evening when she thought of sleeping in the single bed as they did—half the night face to face, the other half top to bottom like a pair of shoes tucked up together because there was more room. She felt clean and calm with him, and they never once spoke of what they did day to day. He took his clothes to his brother's wife once a week, he said, and also his sheets whenever she was planning to stay.

That night, after they had showered together, they stood damp and cool before the window where it opened onto the heat. The city lights were flung out like the cool little snow-drops that grew at home at the base of her mother's hedge; and, stories below, the buildings stuck up around the footwear factory like shoe boxes turned on their ends. And there, over by four or five streets: one lime-green neon lady's slipper stepped out of the head of the main building and flashing, green then green again, danced through the night.

Even when they lay down together—with her eyes opened or closed, it seemed to make no difference at all—she could see the green neon outline of the shoe in miniature tripping along through the dark touching lightly—as if with little kisses—back and forth over the sparse furnishings, clattering around the bare bulb overhead, the corners of the room and his skin, even here now: over the soft hairs of his belly and chest, his hipbones and lean thighs, the long gracefully arching feet, the green outline tripping up his slender calves, up onto the delicate white caps that made his knees. How perfect, anatomy! And life itself! How perfectly the parts of even the legs were held into place. And then her boss stuck his gleaming wet head into the scene and seemed to hover overhead. Why! was *that* what The Terror meant when he declared he would shoot the kneecaps off the prosecuting attorney! or anyone else who stepped in his way! And suddenly it was as if young Monsieur's legs had been blown away. No no, she could not bear it. Then Monsieur had taken hold of her and the immense grinning face of The Terror disappeared.

When he touched her, she was a tangle of gentle comfort behind her closed lids with the green shoe flashing on, then off, then on again, glowing with increasing intensity until finally she felt his breath on her forehead and she saw the image radiating right between her eyes. When she lay there curled under his arm, happy, eyes closed, she watched it fade: very slowly, until it was gone. Once during the night she woke to find the city air especially thick and then she fell asleep again completely at rest with Monsieur's arm across her waist and his breath rising, then falling in her ear.

It was then that her second opulent dream in two nights began. "So," the woman said to her over the large desk. Yellow papers overflowed a metal box off to one side. "So you would

like to buy a cat for the companionship of your old mother,"
she said nodding over her glasses. She sipped from her cup.
"For your aging mother, you say. You are sending her money
then. Every week?" She nodded in life and in the dream. "It
says here that you have a perfectly good dog. You might send
her that. Many persons say these things make a difference in
their lives. They make the difference between breathing and
not, some people say. Perhaps your new boss would conde-
scend to write us a brief note on your behalf or help us in calm-
ing you, do you think?"

The soft hairs on the front of Monsieur's thighs woke her as
they brushed against her own. And then she realized that he
had risen to answer the telephone. The air was so thick now
there seemed to be smoke in the room. She went to the window and thrust it up all the way. Yes yes, Monsieur's friend,
the brush salesman, was calling from that tiny booth at the
bottom of the street; Monsieur brought the telephone to her
side. And then there was a curse from Monsieur. Yes, the
salesman had worried furiously when Monsieur hadn't appeared on the street among the other evacuees. Far below it
was being discussed, even suggested by the firemen: that
some men hired buildings burned down, even their own. The
brush salesman wished sincerely that he had not found him at
home.

Even when Monsieur turned on the light, she could not
see him well. Time seemed to eddy between them as they
drifted down the dark hall, wet towels like a pair of dim
leaves pressed to their mouths. For a moment she felt like a
diagram, completely compressed. She had had the presence
of mind to put on her dress and shoes.

Somewhere the fire escape would be clinging like ivy to the
exterior of the hotel. They had found only the internal stair-
case now. The well ached with an indistinct light. How destiny
carried them down now! in slow motion, past the narrow em-
brasures that had been cut in slivers as if for gun mounts into
the heavy brick and plaster walls.

This was accepted, certainly it must be. If she lost hold of

him she would follow the sound of the smoke being catapulted around in his throat if she could hear it above her own.
How odd, she thought, that there should be no other noise—
not even a crackling. It was as if a blanket had been wrapped
around them both and they were stumbling to deliver themselves up to whatever lay below. She felt like a willow turned
upside down, absurdly, on all its weak swaying little hairs. So
that was what her boss had meant when he said it. Weak-
kneed. No, her boss himself would never have been called
such a thing. All the other clerks had glowed red with embarrassment for her on her first day, and at lunch one young man
had come over to represent the group. They knew very clearly
that she had not done one thing wrong. It was the way of The
Terror. She had had so many hopes for her new life and that
was the day that the hopes had been snatched away.

They both were coughing so violently now that she had run
right into Monsieur when their feet came to a level plane. It
was on the landing where she'd run smack into him and he'd
started to cry. A film slipped between their palms, and together they groped for the door to enter the body of the building again where the air might be slightly more clear. They had
come down only two flights, she was certain of that, and now
they would be on the ninth, crossing over, looking once again
for the external fire escape through the more obscure air.

That week her boss had refused to sign the government papers declaring that she was permanently employed. For three
months he had refused and now there was no hope at all that
her mother might be persuaded to come. She might have had a
chance in the beginning, but already her mother was adjusting to being alone. These things her mother's letters said. Each
day her mother's sadness seemed more natural to her. And
the boss raised up his great hairy arm where he had rolled up
his sleeve: How could he sign them when he had no idea
whether she might, or might not, learn the job? She showed a
few good signs, yes, but how incompetent she seemed. No,
he could not declare to the public officials that she would remain. He could not help it if her visa might be reclaimed.

Overhead pouting through the dark air: a giant white frog, its chest hairs curling out over its circus shirt, arms and thighs bulging, as it lowered, then pressed the bellbar into the sky. "Black Labrador. Filly," it coughed. "Tse-tse fly."

She took off her shoe and, with the sharp heel of it, beat a hole in the small cool pane that her fingers had come up against. She would take the necklace her mother had given her for luck and throw it out. It at least might be saved. Perhaps someone would send it back home. It would keep her mother safe. Or if they should never find her own name, perhaps someone looking up at the building in flames would see an eerie sparkle in the Chicago lights of the firemen and then that person would hear it drop like a winged stone at her feet. Perhaps that someone would carry it through a life suddenly illumined by an enigma: a man and a woman waiting high in a building surrounded by crowds. The chain ran across her fingers, and then she went first, his hand at the middle of her back. She stretched her mouth to the hole she had made. The whole world came in through that pane, cool and refreshing— did she taste a hint of rain?—and went out again.

✖ *To Be Sung*
on the Water

I F the corn weren't so high, the two little girls nestled on the porch swing beside Grandmother might be able to see that house where their six cousins, their Aunt Polly, and their mother's adamant brother Uncle Gilbert live, just two miles up the road. But then, if they could see the house, it would only be a yellow speck; it is such a small place.

From here, Rosie thinks, it might only look like a bright kernel of corn, with its green roof like a leaf laid over the top. Then, too, the windbreak is in the way, off to the right, mysterious and dense, one thick line of trees in all this flat wilderness.

Something frightening and unknown, Rosie thinks, must live in the tangle of old wire fencing at the center of the grove. A horse cart has crumbled to bones in there, the leather seat and bonnet disintegrated to something like the shoelaces of boots. Their mother has gently explained that the pony itself must have died long long ago even before her own time. Surely Grandmother remembers it.

No one looks in the direction of Uncle Gilbert's house anyway. Grandmother is humming a song, little blonde Georgia on one side and Rosie like a brown-headed puppy under the other great fleshy arm. Even when they are grown, Rosie will

think of their grandmother as immense, although Grandmother will be tiny really for the last twenty years of her life.
The little girls don't say a word, just squirm in tight. They are
all three looking at Mother who sits on the porch rail, her back
to one of the white pillars.

Nothing can describe the brilliance of their mother's azure
eyes. Their mother's cheeks are flushed with her zany laughter; her straight white teeth sparkle as she smiles at them. Her
canvas shoes perch together on the top of the rail. Around her
shoulders floats her dark brown hair. Tucked up around the
backs of her thighs, her long turquoise skirt cascades over her
knees and calves, then down to one side between the white
spindles of the porch and a bush of *Rosa rugosa* in full bloom.
Rosa rugosa. Rosie and Georgia have been saying it, over and
over all afternoon, with a laughter bubbling out of them like
little silver bells.

Briefly the little girls glance beyond it: their mother, the
patchy green lawn, and the rusty old pump over the well. The
road winds off into the corn where it sways as if mesmerized.
They do not for a moment look toward the white barn; there
their grandfather, brothers, and father have gone to do unin-
teresting things.

Because she is oldest, Rose knows, people say it especially
to her: "Your mother is so young." Everyone will say to Rosie
as long as her mother is alive, "You look like sisters." The little
girls live far away, in town, hours from here. Too far.

In front of the pink country roses, their mother is so beautiful, both girls will all their lives be awestruck at the
thought—though neither will be less stunning, though in
more conventional ways. When their mother is in a room,
everyone stares with soft eyes at her.

They are watching her talk from time to time, long periods
of it perhaps. Rose forgets to listen, just watching her laugh at
something Grandmother has said. Their mother has a nice figure. Her white blouse dips in small at the waist. Rose will always be smaller, it seems.

Grandmother is running her finger over Rose's shoulder, in

and around the sleeveless arm of Rose's blouse, again and again gently. Air drifts back and forth over her face as the porch swing squeaks, as Grandmother's legs touch down, push off again. Grandmother wears a perfume that is subtle and warm. It seems to float in and around them like a sun-struck cloud that swings over the house.

Now the men are coming up from the barn, Grandpa and Father, great hard men, tall with wide shoulders and keen intelligence. They are talking politics. Even the little girls' slightly younger twin brothers are going on about the election, whether Grandpa should run for the governorship. Even the little girls know what it all means. Georgia leans around Grandmother's white cotton dress, toward Rose, as they swoop toward Mother and away. Georgia rolls her eyes back, and Rose turns her own blue ones in toward the freckles at the bridge of her nose. Why even discuss the election? Everyone knows he will run, and if he runs he will win. Or else he would not have decided at dinner last night to give up his Senate seat. Every one of them knows that.

"Now, now," Grandmother says, catching them at it. She pats both their arms. "Your Grandpa needs every reassurance he can get, especially from his boys." Whether Uncle Gilbert is included in this the girls can not quite make out; all their male cousins certainly are. Their father has always been included in this, even though he and all of them, too, Mama's children, have been raised in a city hours from here, in another state. Two little girls simultaneously poke out their pink tongues. "Boys," Rose taunts, her thumbs in her ears. Even Grandmother laughs. Mother cocks her brow, a flickering at the corner of her mouth.

Father and Grandpa and the twins are trooping past in their heavy boots toward the mudroom at the back of the large house. Grandpa keeps a pair of such boots here for Father, as he never wears them at home. Father laughs toward Mother alone, a bright and sparkling laugh, happy yet deep in his chest. At the back door now, the little girls can hear their brothers hooting at something Grandpa has said, something about the election. "Cock-eyed," Rose says, and Georgia breaks into squeals again.

Then they are quiet. Grandmother is waving toward Grandpa, and Grandpa does the same back. Their hands move in the same rhythm. Grandmother will run the campaign, is already running it; everyone knows that by the silence Grandmother makes in its wake.

"Now now," Grandmother says again. She pats their arms, and with a creak they push off and swing into the future. Because of her, the little girls will never in their lives be truly afraid as many women are. Even in childbirth, some part of them will be held in her arms. In new times, Georgia will be able to speak out in her job; Rosie will become a painter respected in her field.

•   •   •

R o s e is waiting for her lover to come to her in her studio. They have been lovers for nearly ten years, nearly as long as each of them has been married. Every week has been filled with him in some way, by telephone, by mail here in this sunlit room with the shiny vast floors where daily she paints.

Today their meeting will be brief but no less poignant. This week her lover and his wife have had their second child; there is a certain excitement for everyone. Later in the week he will bring the baby here so Rose can meet his first son.

The last time her lover saw her own little boy, he kissed Alfie on the side of his soft brown hair, held him high. "You 'member my daddy?" her little boy asked him, as if his own father had somehow disappeared.

"I remember about him," Rose's lover said, about the man he had only seen once and that from a distance.

"You 'member my daddy?" her little boy asked once again.

"Indeed I do," he said, lifting Alfie up and down in his blue corduroys. "Indeed I do, little man," he laughed, spinning Alfie safely through space, making the sounds a jet plane might make.

Now he has rung the buzzer, and she has opened the door.

He is smiling as he always does, so brilliantly. There is such warmth between them that both their spouses know and choose rarely to say anything.

• • •

MOTHER is in the family room with her feet up for a minute on the footstool. At the far end of the long room, *Gone With the Wind* is propped up in a stand by the ironing board. Father has gone to the office, is working on some new case. Georgia curls over her toenails on the sofa, painting them so light a pink you can not tell which ones she's done except under a bright light. She holds her foot over a piece of cardboard. Even if she did get polish on the sofa, Rose is thinking in the wing chair on the other side of Mother, the spot would only be a rosy petal in among the flowers of the polished cotton cushion.

Georgia and Mother have read *Gone With the Wind* five times together, so far, passing the book back and forth. They make jokes: "Tomorrow is another day," constantly. Rose has not read the book once, though she has seen the movie several times.

Rose is bored. It is very hot outside, and she can think of nothing to do in such heat that would not require misery on her bicycle getting to the event. If she offers to iron, Mother will surely tell the exciting story of her trip to the East Coast again, of how she sold salt water taffy on the beach and met a man who is now a film star. On the other hand, Rose has already heard the story many times. And there is a great deal of ironing.

It's quite true, she will only realize when she is grown: Vivien Leigh looks almost exactly like Mother. When her mother is dead, Rose will remember her mother's face as that of Scarlett O'Hara and once in a while as the quiet mask trying to hide behind the Easter lilies in one photograph.

Mother must be caught off guard to have her picture taken, and then she always looks slightly odd—stiff, quite unlike herself.

Mother is almost through with her iced coffee. Soon she will stand up and begin reading while she irons. If Rose doesn't hurry to make up her mind, the moment will have passed by them.

Now Mother has gone into the bathroom for a second. She is wearing her bright yellow slacks and her white cotton blouse. Mother always brushes her thick hair when she goes into the bathroom. "If you do it each time, it will always be glossy," she says. "Every time, and you will always have exquisite hair."

•   •   •

W H E N he comes into her, he can stay inside forever it seems. This is true of both of them, her husband and her lover, though she only thinks it true of whichever one she is with, at the time. Forever stretches out eternally, just as forever is meant to be.

When her lover is inside her, he sometimes tells her stories. She likes this best on summer afternoons when she turns off her studio air conditioner so that they can slide about in a film of sweat. "Tell me about the tents," she says. "What color were they?"

"They were striped," he breathes into her ear. "White with one blue circular stripe. Like your eyes." His stories are fantastic; and they are true. This is one reason she likes him.

•   •   •

T H E man owned seven mountains, that is the part Rose remembers most, the man who loved her mother and now is a film star. She has seen the famous scar on his chin many times on late night movies. She imagines her mother putting the tip of her fingernail just there under his smile.

•   •   •

A T the funeral of their mother, Rose, already graduated from college, is just beginning to feel Alfie leaping as she carries him in her belly. Her husband stands next to her; and there at a distance, as if at another grave entirely, stands her lover in a dark suit infinitely more tasteful than the perfectly fine one her husband has on. Rose is so upset about the funeral that she cannot get over thinking about the beauty of her lover's suit. She cannot seem to do anything appropriate about this horrific surprise, except now to reflect.

Monday morning again, and her mother is standing directly in front of her, insisting: "If you can't even walk to school by yourself without being terrified, what ever will happen to you?" On days when the edict comes down, her best friend takes a ride with an older brother. She and her friend will meet in the art room and glower silently, staring out past the easels through the large windows, over the good half mile of open autumn fields, toward the edge of town where Rose's mother is no doubt having her mid-morning coffee.

Her mother calls it loneliness, that which she wishes to expunge from Rose. Rose cannot name it. She stands on such mornings before her mother at the front door. Soon she will be outside, then stepping around the corner and going down the long street edged on each side by the excitement of houses and people. But then the town will fall suddenly away. She will try not to think of it until she is directly upon it.

Only as an adult will Rose think of the possibilities of defiance and trickery that other girls might have used with such a mother. Nor will she explain to her mother what it is exactly that frightens her—having to cross that vast open field alone with no one watching or caring what becomes of her. In school now, and later in the world, Rose will always be seen as completely confident.

Now her husband has his hand just beneath her elbow. Perhaps he steadies her lest she might fall straight over, along with their unborn infant, over the edge of the grave onto the gleaming mahogany casket. There she and the unborn Alfie would lie like a fruit basket on a well-polished table, her belly a big sumptuous arrangement, the fabric of her dress swirling around them. And right there surely, below them: her own mother, like a mischievous child, crouched under this banquet on hands and knees, her mother's hair down around a face gone pale white, her own mother laughing wildly.

Perhaps Rose is being melodramatic. Her lover holds her with his eyes, while her husband's arm is around her. There is an element of jealousy in her lover's face, seeing the two of them like that for the first time. Both men steady her as she has steadied them for a number of years now. The two men complement each other so entirely that if either were to leave her, she would leave the other one also. It is amazing that her husband does not notice her lover over there. How could anyone not see his strong face? At least her lover and her husband have managed not to come here on the same plane.

Inside her now as she stares into the grave, her baby swims like a frog this way then that, oblivious that he has just lost his one remaining grandmother. This ancestry is something she cannot share with her lover, although on this day he has come closest to this—anonymously standing in the funeral home, looking onto the dead face of her mother. She will never meet her lover's parents or brothers, nor will her children have knowledge of them.

Now the warmth of her husband's body carries the sweet perfume of his morning shower toward her. Whenever she is sorrowful around him, she undoes the top buttons of his shirt and rests her face at his throat among the wealth of his soft hairs. It is as if her mouth has filled with a sweet mother's milk; comfort washes through her whole body.

It is her lover who stands directly in front of her, though still at an immense distance, gazing across the rows of upright stones and the red flowers dripped onto the landscape. Beside her, Georgia's long blonde hair lifts on a momentary breeze; Georgia takes hold of her hand so hard, Rose thinks, perhaps they are crushing one another's fingers. But then, maybe Georgia is barely touching her hand. The blood may have merely run out of her arm. It may merely have gone to sleep; there is so much numb acceptance. These changes should come with warnings!

Yet there is a sound. Yes, everywhere there seems to be the sound of screeching tires slipping endlessly through water over pavement. If Rose were to look up she would expect to see her mother's umbrella floating there—disembodied and completely startled. It is not what anyone expected for their dear young mother.

Grandmother and Grandpa, Aunt Polly and Uncle Gilbert and all their boys and their wives; Aunt Emily and Uncle Arthur, their daughters still in high school; their own twin brothers home from their last year in college. The whole family has collected, many friends, many of Grandpa's colleagues and friends. Everyone is here.

Including Mother, Rose thinks wildly. Mother is here somewhere, I feel it.

It would be a splendid summer afternoon if it weren't for all of this. The world turns around on its axis, casts a balmy breeze about the whole contorted scene. Black automobiles are parked up and down the winding drive of the graveyard. At the center of the bank of flowers is the loveliest wreath. It is at least four feet across, from one golden yellow rose to the last. Tiny and hammered, a sterling silver horse and rider slip almost imperceptibly over the white ribbon. There is no card; even Aunt Emily has looked for it.

What can it mean?

There are any number of strangers in the graveyard. Every once in a while, one of them looks up to stare into her eyes, perhaps by coincidence.

• • •

"D o I have them—do I have his ears? Were they like this?" Georgia's ears wiggle under her blonde pixie cut.

To their surprise, Mother storms out of the house. The screen door slams shut. "Where is your mother?" their father asks later. Rose and Georgia say nothing. The story of the seven mountains has been to the two girls a secret gift from Mother's past that even their father does not suspect.

Father has not even put down his briefcase. Finally the girls look down at the floor. "Walking," they say.

"Your mother never goes walking right through her dinner. What did you two say to her?"

The girls give an adolescent shrug of their shoulders, to say it: Not Guilty of Hurting Our Mother.

When Mother comes in later she goes upstairs and down the hall, lies on her bed, and says nothing for a long time. "Close the curtain," she does say. "And go out of this room. Do not bother me once until tomorrow morning."

Father, too, is not to be admitted again. Their brothers are already gone off to camp for the week. "What is it?" he asks.

"On second thought," she says to Father, "you come back in an hour or so. These two I don't want to see until Friday."

"Friday!"

"Or maybe Monday after next. And you know what for, you two, so don't go around here saying otherwise. And don't apologize. Nothing will ever make up for it now; you've destroyed it, an entire part of my history."

"What is it?" Father asks, quite alarmed.

"It's between us," Mother says. "Don't ask again."

• • •

A T the appointed hour Rose's lover calls. Sometimes he calls when he says he will, most often he does not; though frequently he contacts her. Sometimes she cannot be home when she says she will be; often she is. This is rather an aggravation, but nothing compared with their not having one another. When they make a decision to meet, they both always show up.

Today her lover says that he has a cold. She can hear that in his voice; it sounds quite uncomfortable having a cold as bad as that.

"Come to the studio anyway," he laughs hoarsely. "We can wear masks."

• • •

H E R husband is reading to her while she soaks in the bath-
tub; they often do this after Alfie has made his way through
storytime, songs, evening snacks, glasses of water, and many
good nights. Her husband has barely begun tonight's chapters
when the telephone rings. It will not be her lover; he does not
call at this time and has no idea what she makes of these moments each night.

Her husband hands her the telephone: "It's Georgia," he
says. And then he laughs, seeing her wince when she takes
the receiver. No matter how many times he has told her, Rose
is still afraid that she will be electrocuted—most particularly
while taking hold of a telephone, when naked, in a tub of
water so frothy it looks like meringue.

But her husband has stopped laughing, and Rose is listening intently now. "I have some bad news for us," Georgia says
very bravely, or so Rose will see it tomorrow. Her sister Georgia has a bravery beyond belief, a mastery of the world.

And what has become of Rose? By day, Rose paints land-
scapes from her childhood; some are abstract. A woman at a
gallery downtown sells them. Or they are put into museums
with beautiful catalogs where she is mentioned beside a minuscule photograph.

But what of this bad message from her sister? What does it
mean?

By tomorrow morning, Rose will find herself elsewhere,
back there, in Grandmother's country. She and Georgia will
have been washed up onto their grandmother's porch in time
for Grandfather's funeral to begin.

•   •   •

R O S E finds herself in her little son's bedroom. He has been
calling out in his sleep. She brushes along his damp cheek,
through his silky hair. His forearm is still round and doughy
where it dips in toward the small bones of his wrist. Her boy
has taken the tiny shirt off his bear so he can rub its fat tummy
while he is going to sleep. She finds herself gently pushing
one furry paw through a sleeve, then the next.

"Believe what you see in your Alfie," Grandmother said. "Very few babies are affectionate like that."

After Alfie has been cuddled and petted, in the last moments before he drops off to sleep, he always prefers to stroke someone else. Rose will never forget her surprise at seeing his tiny newborn hand, smaller than a sand dollar, lifting out from under hers in order to stroke her own skin.

"It looks like Alfie doesn't want to take advantage of you," her lover says.

•   •   •

"W H A T was that story about the seven mountains?" her husband asks on the way to the airport. He sits very tall and stiff in his seat. He has not said much of anything to her this morning.

"Why do you want to know *that* now?"

"I thought it might encourage you," he says.

"Whatever made you think that?" she suddenly snaps, surprising even herself. But she cannot get herself stopped. "Right now you want to hear the story of my mother's near miss at happiness?" Her husband speeds up as he always does when they argue. "Slow down," she says. "It's not worth an accident. I just don't understand your timing that's all."

"I'm sorry," he says bitterly. "Forgive me for not knowing your every nuance."

She taps her foot against the flight bag on the floor.

"Listen," he says, "I'm sorry it happened. I'm sorry your grandfather died. I know how important he was to you. I was only trying to be useful."

"Yes," she says. Yes, she thinks, I suppose you were. My god, she thinks in the fast automobile, what is happening to me. Calm down, she thinks. All she can think about now is how on the day Alfie was born he sent her friends away from the hospital before they could see her.

He didn't even ask me what I thought, she thinks once again. "I'm sorry," she says. "I'm trying to calm down now."

• • •

I N the Statehouse, Grandmother asks Rosie, her confident
one as she truly believes, to carry a silver tray around to all the
people who have been invited to meet them. Across the vast
terrifying carpet she goes, offering the tiny sandwiches.

Later, on the tour of the old fallout shelter, Rosie will cry out,
"But Grandpa can't stand up in it! It's too short. Grandpa will
have to sit down till he dies."

• • •

R O S E will not be able to reach her lover before she leaves the
city. When she does she will be standing in her grandmother's
kitchen in the Midwest, talking from the black wall phone beside the pail of well water and the familiar dipper. Out the back
door she will see the outbuildings, the barn to which she only
once ventured, the empty boots on the back porch, and just
beyond, in the entryway on a railing in a specially vented bag,
Grandmother's old mink coat.

"Hello," she'll say to her lover. "I'm glad I reached you in
time."

"Is something the matter? I thought you were meeting me at
three."

She buries her face in the fur, in the fragrance of her grandmother's skin. "I had to go home," she says into the mouthpiece.

In the background her lover's little daughter is chattering,
his new baby boy howls on his other shoulder. "I thought you
were meeting me at the studio," he says. "You're at home
now?"

"Home home," she says. "Far away. I'm at Gram's house.
My grandfather died yesterday."

"Shush up now, Holly honey, just for one second, then I'll
fix it for you."

She can hear his warmth turning her way again. "Oh,
baby," he says, "I'm sorry. Are you o.k.?"

She can see the kitchen table where the waffle iron still sits.

"I don't know. They used to call it the big house. Suddenly it seems tiny; it's very hard to breathe."

"What about your Grandmother? Is she going to be o.k.?"

"I don't know yet," she says.

"When will you be home?" he asks. "I want to hold you up close. I could kiss your sad eyes."

"Yes," she sighs. "Yes, Tuesday," she says.

"I'll see you then." There is a commotion of children in the background. "Oh fuck," he says, "I forgot all about it. I'm sorry, that's the week of the conference. Are you all right? Hold up, love—I have to go. Her car just pulled in the drive." And then he is gone. There are no good-byes. Rose is sitting on the back room floor, crying hard for her grandmother's life now shattered, a fur coat pressed up against her face.

· · ·

I T feels as if the change in her grandmother is sudden, though it must have been happening for years. Grandmother is not only half her former size; she has lost several inches in height. She now comes up only to the shoulder on Rosie.

Now she and Georgia are sitting with her at the kitchen table. Grandmother stares into her teacup, then she announces, "Gilbert arranged the whole funeral for Grandpa." Grandmother says it almost proudly, referring to her Gilbert's release and recovery.

Rose bursts out before she can stop herself, "Not Gilbert?"

Something pointed and hard has kicked Rose under the table. "Oh," Rose says. "So Gilbert has arranged everything."

No one likes to talk about it: how Uncle Gilbert tried to kill nearly the whole family. It still gives Rose a tight feeling somewhere between her throat and her stomach, like having swallowed something way too hot that won't go down nearly quickly enough. It is better to think about the house for a while: the peeling yellow bungalow down the road that housed so many children, a quaint little house really.

Every holiday, after dinner, as far back as Rose can remember, Grandmother and Grandpa's oldest lay on the sofa, arguing. Silly, inane perhaps, adamant, that was Uncle Gilbert with his face reddened infinitely it seemed, above his white shirt, his light blue pants and suspenders. His shoes sat like firecrackers at the edge of the rug. In the kitchen and in the dining room, grownups could be heard muttering about him. The children used to mimic it:

When is Gil? Going to paint—going to paint—That house? Get off that sofa? Make a go of his farm, of his farm, of his farm? Gil—bert! Gil—bert! Gil—bert!

"It's not the time, Rose, to think about Uncle Gilbert," Georgia interjects gently but firmly.

"Right," Rose agrees quickly. "That's right. I'm sure it will be o.k. We have to think about you, Grams."

"And Grandpa," Grandmother murmurs. "This is the time to think about Grandpa."

Up the lane at the farm. Between Statehouse and governor's mansion. Strolling around the art museum with her grandfather intently listening as she pointed out the spectacular differences in brush strokes and shadings. "I see it, Rose. Yes, Rose," he would say. "It was right there in front of me."

Mostly when he went on, he talked about peculiar things he had seen, animals and people. As far back as she could remember, there sat on his desk a gallon jar of rattlesnake tails a farmer had given him in lieu of payment, a friendly gesture.

Once, after she had just started college and she had come to visit, he looked her straight in the eye and tapped the jar with the back of his fingernail until she shifted uncomfortably. Then he laughed out loud, rather proudly. "Be tough," he said. "Grandma says you're the real thing."

Rose and Georgia remembered hearing the story only once as told to them by their mother. There was a sickness in Gilbert, that was certain, but it seemed intentional suddenly when he began waving the barrel of the loaded shotgun about at Aunt Polly and the crying little children. While the deputy took Aunt Polly and the children into town, Gilbert's old highschool friend, the sheriff, was to take him into the pasture and distract him.

Grandmother and Grandpa, too, were collected by the deputy and put onto a floor of the hotel with the rest of them, under armed guard, until Gilbert was arrested.

Later that week after Gilbert's escape, they would find Uncle Gilbert sitting in a daze, still holding his gun with his dead horses all around him.

"It must have pained Grams and Grandpa a lot to see Gilbie go onto a ward like that," their mother had said to each of them. "Please don't ever mention any of this to either of them."

"Do you remember—" Rose asked with incredulity. "What Grams said once about Uncle Gilbert as a little boy? How he took Mama out to the chicken house and made Mama hold the baby chickens while he cut off their heads with an axe."

"My God," Georgia said. "I had forgotten it."

• • •

O N the day of the funeral, Grandmother is sitting at her kitchen table at the farm. Her hand is circling her mouth as if a cigarette were still between her first two fingers. This is not senility. Not even despair, though the despair is real enough. She has been circling her mouth this way with her hand, off and on in conversation, since she quit smoking twenty years ago. When she quit smoking, oddly enough, Grandmother lost all her excess weight. "I was only eating in preparation for the cigarette," she said, "to build up to the taste."

There on the table is the same blue Fiestaware butter dish. The blue juice pitcher for everyday, and the little roosters in the dishes for sauce. In the dining room in the china cabinet are the stacks of beautifully painted plates, the fine Limoges, and crystal. On the bottom of every one is a sticker with a name on it, written in Mother's hand during the time when the girls were adolescents. Each name directs just who Grandmother said would love each piece, or set, appropriately. The same is true for the paintings and the cherry tables.

In the kitchen suddenly Grandmother is tugging on Rose's

arm. Aunt Emily is trying to explain. Grandmother is to wear
the expensive pink suit Emily has brought her for the funeral.

Rose has never seen her Grandmother cry, except at Mother's funeral. "I can't wear it," Grandmother sobs, holding onto
Rose's arm.

"What is it, Grams?"

It is all quite apparent, Rose is thinking; how could it be
more clear to Emily, or anyone? Grandmother has never worn
this color in her life and would certainly never wear pink to a
funeral. "Grandpa was my best friend," she sobs. "Can't you
explain it to her? Please explain it, Rosie."

Rose looks at Aunt Emily, who has grown heavy under the
eyes though she is slender. "Well, Mother," Aunt Emily
snaps, "you'll have to wear it. I've sent your other things to
the cleaners. They won't be back for a week. I thought I was
doing you a favor."

Grandmother sobs, in Rose's arms. "Grandpa would be
ashamed of me in that," she cries. "He was never ashamed of
me once, Rose, in his entire life. Not ever. Doesn't anyone understand that? You understand me, don't you, Rosie?"

"Of course, I understand you," Rose says. "I understand it
precisely. This is not a fashion show. This is a tribute to Grandpa." Aunt Emily turns on her heel and walks into the downstairs bathroom. For a second, Rose and her grandmother
stand listening to the fiercely running water.

"Grams," Rose says. "Oh, Grams, we're so much alike,
Grams, my grandma." When they are sitting together in the
living room on the sofa, Rose tells her grandmother what she
thinks of Emily's stupidity.

"It is true about Emmy," Grandmother whispers sadly.

"Yes, Grams," Rose says. "That was worse than thought-
less."

"Yes," Grandmother sniffs. "I had three children. One was
cruel, one was crazy, and the other one died." And then she is
crying again, her face in her hands, her white hair softly curled
under Rose's palms.

"Oh, Grams," Rosie says.

"My beautiful, thoughtful, bright, funny one died. And now Grandpapa is gone without me. I never thought he would go without me." She looks up, bewildered. "I mean I considered it, but I never actually thought it would happen. Rosie, Rosie, has it really happened now?"

Earlier that morning Georgia had put her arm around Rose. Aunt Polly had called her during the evening. Grandmother and the aunts had decided it; nothing could be changed. On the morning following the funeral Aunt Emily would be taking Grandmother home with her to live. And, Georgia said, their own plans would be truncated. Georgia and Willy and Rose would drive across the state a week earlier than they'd planned, to Georgia's house, and then Rose in a few days or whenever she was ready would fly to her own home.

• • •

F I F T E E N minutes later, in a pay phone at the station ten miles from the farm, she is charging the call to her private account. Miraculously, her lover answers. "Hello," he says. "Ah," he whispers, "I can't talk now." He clears his throat. "I'm sorry," he says fairly loudly. "You must have the wrong number, dear." Then the phone goes dead. It is as if the rows of corn were marching on the telephone at this rural corner. It is all she can see and this immense sky. When she can think again, she dials and her husband answers. She can hardly keep from crying.

"How's it going, love?" he asks.

"Not too good," she says, gazing out at the field of stalks and ears. She is sighing, "Soon everything will be gone, the whole thing, everything as a child I ever dreamed." Then she stops to catch her breath. "Is Alfie o.k.?" She listens carefully into the telephone for sounds of him. But the television is on in the den, the dishwasher in the kitchen is whirling away.

"He's good," her husband says. "We had a bicycle ride."

"I never thought Georgia would bring Willy along; she's staying in a motel with him. I was counting on being able to spend some time with her. Oh—maybe Alfie should have come, and you. You should be here, too."

"Yes," her husband says. "But you know I'm tied up here. About the rest—I guess that's just about the way these things go. I'm sorry you feel bad."

She leans her head back against the glass of the booth. "Yes," she says, "that is exactly the way these things go. I know that."

Over there is corn, and over there. If it weren't for this crummy little gas station there wouldn't have been a phone like this with privacy for hours.

"Rose—" her husband is saying. "Come back. Hello—Are you there?"

He knows very well that she is still on the phone. It's just that she can't seem to get any words to come out of her throat, it is so swollen with tears. Over the years she has explained this fact to him many times, after the fact. "Rose—" Still he cannot recall the nature of it.

"Rose," he says. "Say something right now or I'm going to hang up. Hello?" he says. "Rose, this is costing several limbs."

"An arm and a leg," she mutters finally.

"What did you say?"

"An arm and a leg, that's how the saying goes," she says hoarsely.

"I know that," he says angrily.

"I guess I'll go back to Gram's now."

"Good," her husband says. "Keep your head up. Soon you'll be home."

"Is Alfie all right?"

"You already asked that. Of course he's all right. What did you think—I'd lose him in a supermarket the moment you were gone? He's fine."

"What's he doing right now?"

"He's watching *Winnie the Pooh*."

"Which one? Oh, let me talk to him. Put Alfie on the phone just for a second."

"All right," her husband says impatiently, as if this were an

unusual request. But Alfie is engrossed. Right now Owl is reciting the story of his eccentric cousin while Pooh and Piglet
are in a flood about to be swept over a waterfall.

"Rosie," her husband says. His tone has changed. "I was
thinking about something you said."

"What was that?"

"'Tenderness.' That's what you said when we were
married."

"Yes?"

"Last night I finally realized, for some time now we've lost
it."

There is no use trying to speak now. She hangs up the
phone, leans her head back again, and stares at the dirty little
gas station windows, the encrusted gas pumps, the long black
hoses that snake the broken pavement.

Yes, out there, just across the road, across that flowing field,
and that one, the horses are running, somewhere, at the edge
of a cemetery she hasn't seen for years in another inland state.
There the corn rises up against a stone wall, the only one she
remembers ever seeing in this part of the country.

• • •

H E R E it takes place, in a cheap funeral home rather than in a
church—so Uncle Gilbert has determined. Grandmother, in
her pink suit, is so small in her grief that she doesn't truly
seem to know where she is. She has never been here before;
that is a certainty. A gigantic plastic cross rides the back wall.
The music is piped in from a tape machine. But the casket that
Grandmother has chosen with Georgia and Aunt Emily is
beautiful even in these surroundings.

Georgia sits beside Rose. Their brothers' and their father's
dark shoulders are lined up with the other pall bearers' in another pew. Here are the aunts and uncles gathered again. All
the political chums and even some of the opponents out of
sheer respect, and Grandfather's successor. Georgia's little
Willy is perched alertly beside her in his grey summer slacks
and jacket, in his first tie.

Perhaps Georgia is the only one in the family with her head screwed on straight, just as everyone has been saying for a long time, even though she left her first husband when Willy was three months old. Yes that was certainly something unforeseen; how that very professional man had started uncontrollably to drink and brawl at whatever was in the way once his son was born.

Willy is the one bright spot in the entire weekend. If she had only brought Alfie, Rose thinks, she would not have felt quite so bad. There would have been two little boys to snuggle up to a bereft Grandmother on the sofa.

The preacher is tall and slender with his beige hair slicked back. When he opens his pink lips, out comes a rolling voice that acknowledges no one, something Rose has never seen or heard before in this part of the country. "We are called," he says into the microphone, "We are called to the Kingdom but once. And when we are called we have no choice but to give Him the reins."

The music is a tape, Rose keeps thinking. There down the row from Georgia are Grandfather's friends, bowing their heads. There has been no eulogy. Not one word, so far, has been mentioned about Grandfather's career, not one word about the books he wrote about nonviolence, the peculiar laugh he had, not one word of acknowledgement to Grandmother.

It was not so many summers ago when she heard it on the news. She was in the car with Alfie, driving to the beach. Her husband was at home working; "Sure," he'd said scornfully, "I'll come along to the beach, but if I do I plan to sit in the car and read." Her ears had perked up when she'd heard about the prison riots in her grandfather's state. Three guards had been killed, another held by the prisoners. Her grandfather had walked into the fray, they said, unarmed, "accompanied by a pair of Quakers." Three days later, she heard from Grandmother that he'd come out. As Grandmother said, "We came up with a bargain." The riot had stopped. Certain moneys had been diverted for the housing the prisoners had requested and to new and mandatory training programs. He wore a bandage on his right arm.

The hired minister stumbles on. How low we sink, Rose thinks. We might all be the same, if you were to look at the world through eyes like these. In the end, she thinks, are we or aren't we the same? Does spirit and generosity and direction not mean a thing? Rose is tapping her fingers on her thigh. The preacher has taken a further turn toward dramatics. He has put on his eyeglasses; he is banging his fist on the pulpit. He steps toward the casket.

Suddenly Grandmother sitting in the front row with her children, with Uncle Gilbert and Aunt Polly, with Aunt Emily and Uncle John, leans forward as if speaking to the minister himself. "Not yet?" Grandmother asks anxiously.

The man looks at her blankly for a moment through his glasses. Rose two pews back can hear Aunt Emily curtly whispering, "No, Mother. They won't shut the casket, not until we go. You'll have plenty of time."

"Aunt Rosie—" Willy leans toward her over his mother.

"Shush, shush, dumpling," Rosie says, stroking his hand on the lap of Georgia's gray dress.

"Mama," Willy says in his high voice next to Georgia. "That man is funny. What is that funny man doing?"

"Willy," Georgia whispers, smoothing the crease down his little leg. She puts her arm around him, but he shrugs it off.

"Mama," he whines loudly. "What is that funny man doing up there?"

Brusquely Georgia stands and makes her way down the row guiding Willy ahead of her. For Rose, a chasm opens up just beside her. The pastor goes on, calling out in singsong tones for Jesus to enter their lives. Grandfather's first name is being used like a calling card.

A brush salesman would have been better, Rose thinks, staring at the back of Uncle Gilbert's thick neck. Will she stand up and walk out of her own grandfather's funeral? She shifts in her seat miserably. If only she had left when Willy and Georgia did.

The preacher lifts his arms. The people are to join in with the tape and sing a vaguely familiar hymn as written out on a mimeographed sheet. He runs his hands through his hair again, holds them out over the edge of the pulpit as they are to begin. Even over the top of the recorded music, there are footsteps coming through the speakers as Willy and Georgia leave. Then over the pastor's pleading tones again comes Willy's high voice: "Mommy, what is Grandpa *doing* in there?" The pastor's face is pale.

Their feet swoosh up the hall; and then the metal lever on the door creaks down, the door whisks open, and then shuts. Through the windows comes the sound of feet on the walk, and then off in the distance the melodic squeak of a swing, a child's high voice describing with certainty the heights and speeds he would like to attain.

The pastor holds his chin in his hands, elbows still on the podium, staring out over the crowd. He has circles like donut holes around his eyes that she had not noticed before. His hymnal snaps shut. He turns and abruptly sits down in the chair just back of the pulpit. How oddly his body tilts on the gold velvet cushion, and then he is groping awkwardly under his thigh. His face reddens deeply as he maneuvers it out from beneath him, his Bible. When he presses it onto his knee, his eyes snap shut with a finality that will be the last thing Rose remembers about this service for her grandfather.

• • •

O P E N fields aren't all bad, her lover said once. I remember one. Yes, she said. He had made love to her once in the middle of a meadow unshielded for nearly as far as she could see by even a tree or a coat. She could not close her eyes, pressed like that between sky and earth, the two of them in between, their backs arching; the beautiful landscape, a Turner painting, whirling around them in the heat.

"You have to be more alert to things that flourish," he said on that day. "More things are flourishing every day than disintegrate. That's the way it is."

"Yes," she said.

"And look at us. We haven't gone anywhere bad in all these years. What was the likelihood of that? And your husband— he's been good for you, too. Alfie. You have heaps of goodness all around you. To say nothing of your career."

"No," she says. "I've always done well. I mean, yes. It isn't *weltschmerz*, not right now anyway. It's *angst*."

"Oh, that," he laughs. "I love you more than a little bit. That's all that takes."

"I know," she says. "I know that. Thank goodness."

• • •

S H E is in her nightgown now, and here is her Grandmother in the hall, looking lost, looking for towels for her Rose.

"It's all right," Rose says, "I got some, Gram. I already sneaked in for a shower; I'm ready to sleep now." Everyone else has gone to motels, even Emily who had planned to stay with Grandmother has thought at the last minute to take a room. Georgia is in her motel with Willy so as not to disturb Grams tonight. Rose is glad of this time alone with her. Tomorrow Aunt Emily will take her away from this place, these her things.

"Rose," Grandmother says, small and bewildered. "Where has everybody gone?"

"They've gone to motels, Gram. They'll all be back tomorrow."

"No," Grandmother says in a high voice. "I don't mean them. Everybody else. You know. You know who I mean. I don't know how they could be here one minute and be gone the next. I've never understood that. Do you understand it, Rose?"

"No, Grams," Rose says. "I have never understood one terrible thing about it." Her little grandmother has her head on Rose's chest. Rose will never in her life forget the lovely fragrance of her grandmother's skin, especially when her grandmother wears no perfume. When Alfie was born, each time she nuzzled his fuzzy baby hair, she was startled with pleasure: there was the scent of her own grandmother given to her once again.

Now she holds her grandmother so tightly. "I'm afraid, Rose," her grandmother says finally, her blue eyes lifted up under her snowy hair. What miracle this brilliant white after all the color it once held.

Rose holds her small form against her breasts. "Me, too," she says. This voice is not her adult voice; it startles her and her grandmother also. This is a voice torn straight out of Rose's childhood. "Me, too, I'm skeered, Grams."

Her grandmother smiles up at her, and then she laughs just a little. "Better come on then, my Rosie," she says, "better get into bed with your Gram."

Her grandmother does not, under such stress, forget and say what she always said to her as a child. Still the phrase hangs there as if one of them had spoken it.

"He was never a bear, Gram," Rose says.

"Because I made you all keep quiet, that's why, Rose."

"Grandpa wasn't bear material," Rose says. "And we never were quiet."

"That's true," Grandmother says, fiddling with the sleeve of Rose's nightgown.

"The little boys jumped on the end of the bed, and Georgia even wet it. He never once growled."

"That's true enough, darling, it is."

Tonight Rose will lie in the mahogany double bed in her grandfather's place, her eyes looking into the dark, trying to see what her grandmother has seen each time she has waked in the night, the tall bureau, the large round mirror over the vanity where she saw herself change from a great beauty into a beautiful heavy woman into a frail small elderly person. There needn't be light for Rose to see the tapestry seat of the vanity stool, the lace curtains lifting on the breeze as it sweeps in over a field of corn swaying as far as anyone can see. The crickets sigh themselves to sleep in a land so vast she cannot contain the thought of it.

She holds her grandmother all night, and her grandmother

sleeps quietly. Rose strokes her arms, the sides of her face, the beautiful shrinking form, thinking of her grandfather's long thin hands.

In the morning Grandmother is carried away like a portrait, waving there from the window of Aunt Emily's back seat, out of her own life. At this time, Rose thinks and Grandmother thinks it, too, Rose can tell from the way they cannot pull their eyes from one another at the last. They will never see one another again. Later Rose will remember this feeling as yet another of their closenesses. It will be sad, but it will seem fitting that this all will have been true.

· · ·

I N a small cafe on the way home, in the middle of nowhere, as both of them call it, the absolute middle of nowhere noplace, Rose and Georgia stop for lunch. Willy is hungry, is grouchy, is half-asleep, has had his blond little head stuck out from his carseat in a scowl for miles.

In the cafe, men shoot pool, lean in their undershirts against a bar and make jokes. When the two strangers and the boy come in, every one of them smiles. Their dinner is before them so quickly.

But, in the middle of the peaceful moment in the little booth in the country cafe, "No no no," Willy is crying out. "No taters."

"Stop," Georgia is saying. "Stop, you wanted potatoes, you specifically wanted potatoes, that's what you said. Look here's the catsup. We'll make a little face on them."

"No no no," he cries, and then he has picked up one and flung it across the room.

Now Georgia has gone out with Willy kicking under one arm, without lunch, to the car; and Rose sits alone. She can hear her nephew bawling all the way from here, and her sister is talking in a fiercely restrained voice. "You are not going to behave this way in public. This is not the way to behave."

"Go away," Willy yells.

"It's been a long long day. You did so well, and now can't you just hold on a little bit longer." But Willy is crying and yelling. "Willy, you are driving me absolutely mad."

"Go away," Willy screams. "Go away, Mommy, go away."

"If you don't stop screaming that—" Georgia stops midsentence, then begins again, very slowly. "Don't ever say that to me again, William, don't you ever, ever say that to Mommy again."

"Go away, go away from here, Mommy. Go away"

There is a long silence. Rose can almost imagine Georgia grinding her teeth. Then Georgia laughs. "I'll have you arrested. The sheriff will come and lock us both up." She laughs a little wildly. "I think they might lock us up *today* for that matter," Georgia says with exuberance. Willy shrieks with delight. But her voice is dropping. Willy giggles and then is quiet; Georgia is talking to Willy, but mostly she is speaking to herself.

When Rose goes back to the car, she has packages of food wrapped up for them. Willy eats his potatoes, soggy with catsup, smearing them onto his carseat and singing at the same time.

"Don't sing, Willy," Rose says, staring back from the passenger seat at his red-smudged face in the center of the backseat. "For Christ's sake, you might choke. Don't sing while you eat, Willy, please."

"Let him sing, for God's sake," Georgia says, pulling onto the long flat road unreeling before them. "If he chokes, we'll get it out."

"Right, you're right," Rose says. "I hope."

"He probably won't choke. Will he?" Georgia says looking briefly back at him.

In the back seat, Willy looks wide-eyed at them, a french fry lifted into the air, his mouth open wide enough for an artichoke.

"It's o.k.," Georgia says. "Willy. Eat and then sing. Be happy. It's o.k. Aunt Rose is here with us after so long away. And we are going, thank God, straight home."

"It looks like fierce rain," Rose says, "let's drive carefully."
And then Willy is asleep. The radio plays music they both have
loved in college, while the windshield wipers whisk back and
forth.

.   .   .

A L L Rose can think of now is the story of the seven mountains, thanks to her husband who has a way of doing these
things. This is something she had no wish to think about.

Between the two of them, Georgia and Rose piece it together. Mother must have been very young. She could not
have been more than sixteen, and he was perhaps twenty-
three. The sand swept out and out along a vast open sea, the
likes of which she had never before seen. Bright umbrellas
arched like tents over the beach. When she opened her mouth
the first time in the water, the brine of it startled her enough to
make her exclaim.

Oddly, neither of them remembers much about the seven
mountains. Once Mother went to dinner at the boy's house,
the boy who become a film star. A man met them at the door,
clearly a servant.

Both of them remembered one particular conversation in
the same way:

"And did he— Did he—"

"Yes," Mother says finally. "It was the most beautiful summer of my life."

"You made love to him?"

"You must never tell Daddy," she says.

"Why didn't you stay with him then?"

"I was only sixteen. It didn't seem like it could be right already, a decision like that so early in my life."

"But Daddy."

"Yes, Daddy," she says. "He started flying his plane over
the house. Figure eights, all of that. I had pretty much given
up on my friend. He seemed like a failure to himself, he said in

his letters; he could never ask me after all this time. He was a flop in the movie business, could not even get a part as a bellhop."

"Not really!" they exclaim in astonishment, not yet knowing the disappointment upon which successes are made.

"And don't feel sorry for Daddy," Mother insists. "All his life he's been mourning for his old Louisiana love."

"*Daddy* had a girlfriend in Louisiana?" one of them had asked her. "He flew an airplane over the house?"

And then, with great seriousness, together they had asked, "And what about Grandmother, what did *she* think?" About their grandmother's new situation, neither will be able to talk for several days.

No one had ever known what Grandmother had thought about the courtship. No one had ever said, and neither one of them had dared to ask, especially after Mother was gone. The one thing they could recall was hearing Mother say how Grandpa had responded to the aerial stunts over his farm. "Now flying," Grandpa said, "seems normal enough a maneuver but hearing that boy kiss is like hearing a cow pull its foot out of the mud."

"Daddy?" the girls said.

"Elegant Daddy is not much of a kisser," Mother said. "As far as kissers go. He has other qualities," Mother said abstractedly. "He has great stamina in life. Yes, great stamina is your father's way. Not everyone has stamina. Well, you'll see what I mean."

The land has begun a bit to rise and fall under the heavy clouded sky. In the back seat, Willy stirs a little, and the two of them lower their voices. "Think of it," Rose says. "She had the best moment of her life at sixteen. The rest was downhill."

"At least she had one," Georgia says. "That's more than I can say."

"Your husband had a few redeeming features, you said,"

"Right," Georgia says sardonically.

"Right," Rose goes on, returning to what can safely be said.

"But, Georgia, at sixteen Mother couldn't have even known what best was."

"And after that, except for us, she had no one. She didn't have a job," Georgia says. "She never really went anywhere. All she did was read."

"One romance with you a hundred times."

"And Daddy, it doesn't say much for Daddy," Georgia says.

"Oh, Daddy," Rose says. "Daddy is a stick, a complete stick. Funny, but cold."

"Oh no," Georgia says. "Daddy isn't cold, not Daddy."

"If you're not his daughter he is," Rose says with conviction. "This is not charm we're thinking about. Think about him alone with her. He doesn't light up."

Georgia looks over from behind the wheel of her new car. "What do you mean, 'light up'?"

"Light up. I mean, light up. Ignite from head to toe starting with the eyes, spontaneously, in response to another human being, especially his *wife*. Maybe he lit for somebody else, or anybody. Who knows? Not for Mama though."

"Good God," Georgia gasps. "I never once thought of that in my life. He was so warm to me."

"Different sort of warmth entirely."

"Oh my God," Georgia says. "I've been looking for the wrong thing."

"Ha!" Rose laughs. "And I found it. Daddy exactly, that's what I've got."

"At least you've got someone. Two! You've got what's his name."

"When I can get through his wife's radar screen."

"You could at least have told me he was at Mama's funeral, Rosie. I could at least have had one look at him."

"Are you kidding?" she laughs. "In front of the family?"

"Henry Miller," Georgia says then, with incredulity, staring into the rain-drenched road.

"What about Henry Miller?" Rose says.

"Fitzgerald and Henry Miller were her favorite authors; she told me after I got to college."

"Henry Miller!"

"My goodness," Georgia says. "I wonder if that was supposed to be a secret."

• • •

I T occurred to Rose once while holding to the strap of a sub-
way car. It seemed so obvious: Andrew Wyeth was surely the
only living being to have understood that moment when she
stood at the edge of the field and felt the top of her head fly off
like a rocket and whirl into the sky, how it happened each
time, just when her foot touched down on the abyss that
stretched out between the edge of town and the distant
school. He had surely understood the distance between two
points. And now he had come out with them: his portraits of
Helga.

• • •

B U T they have stopped the car, here where they have not
been in so long. After all it was on the way, nearly. Willy is
awake in the back seat and anxious to get out. Here is the road
to the cemetery where their mother is buried. When last Rose
saw it, it was an open stretch of land that swept from the high-
way on the edge of town all the way out through fields to the
horizon almost.

Now the town has moved in on it. There are new houses not
a mile up the road, many of them in similar pastel forms. Trees
have grown up around them, have had time to grow. Still the
horses run in the pasture off at the end of the little stone wall,
the intervening picket fence. The ground has been broken in
patches for more graves. They will get out of the car; and over
there, soon, they will stand at her grave and be swept back.

It has truly begun to rain now. The windshield wipers go
back and forth as the car moves through the curving paved
lanes. They have opened their doors; Willy is released to run
among gravestones and exercise his lungs. Over there the
small trees have grown up. Vast white heads of tree hydrangea
hang down in the rain over her stone. Even from here, they

can see her name as they approach. "My God," Georgia says. In an instant, a red rash has gone up over her throat.

"What is it?" Rose says before she can realize what she has seen. A rectangle of water sits where the mound of grass should be. Their mother's grave has sunk completely into the earth, and in it water has its way.

Rose can not say a word. She stands with her hand somewhere in the air near her face, staring at the dim reflection of clouds and bushes in the grave.

Georgia's voice scratches with her anger, "They are responsible for keeping this place up. We pay them an annual fee."

"It's actually sunk," Rose says. "It's completely sunk. How long can it have been this way?"

To say that she is crying is an understatement. She has even raised both fists into the air as she walks away. She is so outraged she cannot even see herself in her grief. There are so few graves.

But at the grave of their mother, her sister has not moved. Georgia stands over there, aghast.

Why am I on my knees here in the middle of this cemetery? Rose thinks. Surely her sister asks this question about Rose as she glances over toward her. There Georgia stands, a rash growing up over her chest as it has since they were little, whenever she's been terribly distraught. Red specks cross her sternum, each one her way of releasing tears, there are so many that Rose can see them clear over here. So much love goes between the two sisters that they do not need to say a word. And there is Georgia's son, Rose's nephew at the grave of his unseen grandmother, in his yellow slicker. Georgia has made him put on his boots.

"Mommy," Willy says. "Why is your mama sleeping in that little lake?"

And then she is speaking very softly to him.

· · ·

I N the beginning she used to ask her lover quite frequently, "Why do you need me? Why me?"

"Why do you need me?" he would say, smiling at her. "Have a little faith."

• • •

A N D here, this one grave, belongs to a young man who lived not far from them, a boy not much older than they were. According to the date it was one of the first to have gone in after her mother. Only a year later, a little more; so long ago now.

She remembered him, a face only for this dead one, who had lived there just on the edge of the vacant lot where the earth dropped off into field and flatland, the autumn remnant of grain already harvested. Perhaps her mother was right after all, perhaps it was loneliness. Still she thinks it only an horrific fear of those open, unending spaces: that field. And on it, among the dirt clods and stubble she moved, feeling like an upright stick, a pencil in progress across an asbestos world. My god how stringent her mother used to be. And how rarely this fact has occurred to her in all these years.

Georgia is speaking again as she walks Willy back and forth through the rows. Rain is glancing down over them all. Oblivious, Georgia is running her hand through her own wet hair. Her dress is soaked through, but the air is warm. On Rose the rain feels good.

"That's a place where many people from many religions go after they die. Their spirits go there, I guess. It's very hard to explain."

"What's a 'sprit,' Mommy?" Willy asks.

"Oh, I don't really know, Willy," Georgia says with weariness in her voice. "It's time to get some exercise now. Let's do some running while we can."

"What's a 'sprit,' Mommy?"

"Oh, Willy, it's something you can't really see. It's who you are in your deepest sense. You'll understand it better when you get older."

If only these revelations could be spoken from generation to generation. If only her mother had tried to help her see what she'd come to know.

Here was this boy for instance after all this time coming back to her as if actually seen: his clean dark hair, slicked back to one side, his sharp knowing eyes. Why couldn't her mother do that? At least, she could have remained a memorable face, not something replacable by photographs. This boy's was a face that did not smile but that looked on with a certain interest. He was not beautiful, not really hard or handsome. He was vivid, a sort of young movie star on a motorcycle, the sort her own mother might have noticed.

He was not unlike the movie star who had grown up owning seven mountains. The boy had had one, too, very shining chrome and black leather, a motorcycle that would take him to his death. Vaguely she remembered knowing, by letter perhaps from an old friend. Oddly enough, she had seen him so frequently, yet never once had she heard his voice.

Her mother had only one friend, Rose thinks now. And that friend had lived across the street from this boy. Perhaps her mother's friend had actually watched her cross the field. It seemed unlikely though, didn't it? Did her mother know in that small town—only as a child had it seemed like a city—that the boy stood there every day carefully polishing those long silver tubules? For Rose, he was just as much a part of that ritual her mother had imposed upon her as the field had been though until now she had never realized it.

There the boy stands, very tall at the house at the edge of the field, much older than she was—or so it seemed then—only four years at most—a senior perhaps or just beginning at the college. It is hard to remember.

She would have been too young, too intellectual for him— in just those few years difference, too much another generation, her wire glasses not at all his leather jacket as he polished the chrome each morning on his motorcycle as if he had no where to go but here in the driveway at the edge of the world.

Perhaps her mother and her friend had designed the whole thing, an intended meeting between the boy and herself. It was her mother made her wear such a daring bikini to the pool all the summer before, rather an embarrassment. "You have such a good figure."

All she had seen was the great open space of her trepidation. There he stands. Still she can see him polishing the already—why did she never notice it—they were *already* gleaming: the exhaust pipes at the side of his bike. It was not ostentatious, nor was he—not radical in his appearance. A clean face, not really boyish perhaps. That is what set him apart, perhaps he was intimidated by her, though younger, already known for her drawings in the school, a peculiar play she'd written. Who recalls? On those days she went by him, blinded, thinking hateful things about her mother, the arch enemy who would have her daughter separated from her friends for her own experiments in loneliness.

And then inexplicably, her mother had sent her away to college, to summer school, on the very afternoon of her graduation. An absurd command, even her father had thought it so then. Her former boyfriend had already been gone to college two years, had gone away chaste. Why had her mother done such a thing?

If she had stayed for the celebrating night she might have fallen into someone's arms, been held away from that loneliness, that edict, that she would go away from that town on the very day of her graduation with no parties, no lying down in a nakedness for the first time in bare arms in a blanket in a field, under terrible unforeseen stars, in the balm of departures, perhaps her whole character would have been different. Perhaps she herself would have married a different man.

But brief kisses only it would be for her then, on that night, and then her friends falling away as she looked once through the automobile's windows once at her hometown receding never again to reappear.

Not long after that, her father would move into a practice in another town, hours away; the twins would graduate there, she would marry a man from the East and go there to finish her own college education. Two men she would meet from the

East, one already married. Then their mother would be struck
by a car and be buried among strangers. Right here. Buried in
a grave so heavy that it would sink right out from under her.
Yet here was this boy, brought up to stare each day over this
flatland, somehow nearly an acquaintance, a reassurance to
Rose finally, perhaps as he was meant to be.

Perhaps her mother had forced her to go away that day so as
not to have such a night as she herself had had among foreign
roses and dunes, a night that she could never again see realized in all her life. Could there have been that kind of benev-
olence in her mother's thinking?—in a woman so hard as that?
Rain washed down through Rose's hair, seemed to cloud up
the sky.

And when she and Georgia were little and the boys had not
yet been born, her mother had confided in them, she had tried
to leave their father, riding by train all night with the two of
them tucked in at her sides, reading books to them whenever
they woke up. It was so long ago, it seemed. Grandmother
had sent them all home; Grandpa was running for his Senate
seat.

It was not until last year, long after Mother was gone, that
their father had said to them, "Your mother, you can't know
what she put up with for me."

And Georgia had pressed him, until he said it. "There were
rats," he said. "You were little, I was in school, and there were
rats."

"We had rats in our house!" they had cried.

"I was so busy," he said, "I forget it myself."

Had her mother's friend known all along this awful story
from her mother's life? When her mother was killed and Rose
supposed the young man at the edge of the earth was riding
toward his own later death, what had her mother's friend
thought then?

It has taken her over ten years to know this, and she only
admits it at this moment. Sitting here on this grave she has
seen this boy for the first time. In these dead dark eyes was
manliness, indifferent yet engaged. She can almost see life's

short fall from his shoulders, the spray of young hair between upper arm and chest wall, the curls that must have grown across his nipples, his face, and then her chin on his shoulder, pressed up against the moist side of his neck. Was that what her mother had wanted for her? What does it mean?

If she had met her lover first she would have married him. But then, he was already married. For years she has not been able to admit it: she prefers him, takes as much of him as she can get of him. Drinking it up in spare moments. It has been the sheerest joy and misery; and at home it has been a most comfortable death. If either were to leave her, she would leave the other. And if she were to leave both of them?

Perhaps she would have her silver fantasies, perhaps only that.

• • •

S T I L L it is raining, falling down over the flattest, most beautiful empty dark black land you have ever seen. Her mother's grave is sunken into the earth. When the sun rises, nothing anywhere in sight can conceal it. Only the silhouettes of horses will cut the horizon. And there the broken arch of a town. Rain comes down, does not cease. The grave is so sunken even now that perhaps the coffin has dropped out underneath and been swept into some vault of the underground, carried on an unearthly current through rapids and infested streams.

She had forgotten what rain was like in this country, the sky breaking open, a sulphurous lightning burning its way through loam-scented air. Sound drives down the soil as much as the rain. Everywhere is water in rivulets. Filling even her mother's casket, hair and limbs waterlogged and floating. Is there no sanctity even in nature? How could her own grandparents have turned them away? Someone is crying it out, hoarsely in the distance. The word floats up over the tiny people wandering among insignificant tombs. She looks up startled, her own mouth open, hollering. The cry wends its way from the depths of her chest, burns out of her throat. What was her mother's greatest fear? "Water!" Water in every cell bursts. She could not go out on open water even in a covered boat.

Her sister's brow is furrowed, almost in terror, as she looks back at this stranger. Her sister's body does not turn from the grave yet her face cannot stop staring at Rose who can not stop screaming the word.

Her whole body has begun somewhere to hurt. "Water!"

Tiny splashings lift in the background. "Water!" her nephew rejoices, echoing her. Then, each time, comes his lively response. His black rubber boots kick up beneath the yellow slicker in the shallows that hold a grandmother deep in its locker. "Water!" Rose screams.

"Water!" his high, lovely voice lilts.

Then she has truly startled herself. Maybe her mother did have something for herself. Perhaps that boy, that young man, was sleeping with her mother, just as she herself sleeps with her own lover. That was something so valuable in her life that, even to her sister, it could not be explained. Perhaps her hard mother had asked that boy to watch over her each time she crossed that field. Maybe she had asked him to watch over her awkward, frightened daughter Rose.

On the winding road in the rain, hanging off the hand pump at the well, running up and down the aisles of stonework now, Willy dances. He turns circles in his black rubber boots and yellow slicker, finally set free. "Water!" he sings. His eyes are full of fortune as he shifts it with his feet, this beautiful substance, shimmering in reflection of his golden coat. He leaps, kicks it up: God's great gift in this long, long weekend of inexplicable occurrences. Here it is: a splendid summer afternoon of moats and boots during Aunt Rose's unexpected visit from the East.

On Star Street

MRS. ESSIE came to the window and looked out. No, she did not, Mrs. Essie said. No! she had never once come to the window in her life. Nor would she in the Hereafter. There were no windows in the Hereafter excepting for the one that looked out from the ultra-deluxe living room of our Lord Jesus Christ, looked out over the hillside where Mrs. Essie's relatives lay in the mist making like frogs their limbs all akimbo or whatever it was. The word escaped her now, it did, and all those other words about double-backed beasts and Elizabethan toads. She did not need to say a one of them to herself, nor out loud!, to know what it was that her relatives had done to her—though it had been tidy, kept to a metaphor at least—by putting her into this place. A rest home. And on Star Street. What a kick. What a screw.

The entire sky had gone pink over her double-jointed bed, out her window, over the town—what was left of it now that whatever it was was a matter of memory logs and files on the brain. In six days and nights she had lost one entire suburb and could not get it back. The nurses—nurslings, she called them—were absolutely no use, though they seemed to like her just fine, better perhaps than most of the others, though she had not yet met the others and did not intend. Did not resolve to watch them pop off as the Almighty reached out the

window with his elongated swatter and hammered them
down. Yes, religion had grown to a factor in her life. The priest
came and went prepared always for the worst in his black shirt
and the little white collar that let you know whether he'd
washed and had a change. You could never be too sure with a
black shirt the way it covered the dirt. She had had a lot to
mourn over herself, yes yes she had, but that was not to get in
the way. Life was the thing. Yes indeed. Whoa, the sky had
gone pink, yes, blue now and turning toward gray.

Oh, rhetoric, what was the use? She was slowing down.
Was not. Yes she was. And had. The day began slowly. How
did it begin? She would not think of that. One mean little piece
of toast cut on the bias. She could not tolerate that. Though
she had once tried: The crumbs had been severed, she declared, catty-corner and fell onto the buds of her tongue with
an indifference that did not occur if you cut the bread right:
once straight down the center and then once straight across at
the one-third line carefully measured down from the butter-
crusted top.

She would explain it to them, the importance each morning of consecrating her bread, placing the Cross on it and cutting it through. There are not so many things one can do in
one life to set one at ease, and if this now was one she had
found in her, how many?, innumerable years—She chose
not to count. Her age was nothing to her. Not 63, 65, 87 years
had changed her whole life. Yes, it meant quite something to
her to see the little cross on the golden slices every morning.
It was one of those things you didn't tell on yourself. Especially if you had adopted the face of an heretical bloke
about town, as she liked to think.

The whole town swept out from the foot end of her bed
like a drive-in picture show her great niece had once taken
her to. There in one immense rectangle, a wilderness had
roamed about the main character's face as if he had just bit
into an apple and swallowed half a worm—only to find it the
sweetest taste ever before known to himself. Mrs. Essie sitting bolt upright in her great niece's ancient Cadillac had

waited for the scream but no, the girl on the screen was
fainted away dead as earth. At this both she and her niece
had turned toward the popcorn—this Mrs. Essie remembered in particular. A kernel of it had attached itself for over a
week to Mrs. Essie's artificial teeth.

It was true: A whole life could be centered around the smallest of signs. Mrs. Essie would lie still in her bed and say not a
word about her desire. There was her toast. Cut onto the bias
it was, once again. Where was the upright for the Body, where
would they attach His tender little arms? Perhaps they had
taken Him down and He, even now, was at large. Nurse
Barnes was offering up the jellies which would be very slippery round about the tongue; the jam wherein a whole fruit's
life must be contained; and the marmalade, oh the bitter embellishments of experience, declared right there on the peel.
From a little wicker basket that dangled from nurse's arm the
condiments were conveyed. Each of the packets was decorated with the painting of the fruit it contained, perfect little
portraits as each must have looked when it was alive. She had
forgotten completely how she had meant to phrase it, the unusual request—for she had never before heard it said. Not
anything like it. And what was the question? Whom would
she ask? My how time seemed to dawdle then soar. It had
something to do with the meaning of bread.

✖ *Actual Oil*

I

O u t in the blue-green rolling farm country, nestled in tight near the elbow of the state woods, in the lap of the Wapsipinnicon Valley, the long dirt lane burrows among heavy corn, and then drifts into spacious grazing for sheep. Fat gray and white tufts of wool waft here and there, as if on diminutive stone feet over the blue-black soil and up to the electric fence. There, out of a brief buttercupped yard, popping with red and white chickens, the sky-blue farm house rises up two and a half stories square.

Picture them, three women: farmers all, with their teaching degrees—Mother Minto, still small, pink-beautiful, and dark-haired, resting in wicker furniture on the glassed-in porch along with her elder sister Aunt Winn, and Mother M.'s own grown-up daughter Maizie Lee. All had returned to the Minto name. Aunt Winn braided her life-long auburn hair from its end at the back of her knees, up into a great luscious coil. An exotic trait, the hair turned there like a quiet python at the back of her kindly head.

In and around the tributaries of the Wapsipinnicon River, especially there in the slightly hillier territories fed by Wild Creek, Maizie Lee Minto was noted to be a pretty woman who sported corn-yellow hair, long like her mother's and aunt's. Sometimes in the yellow-green background of the spring season, Maizie's slate blue eyes took on a shadow of aquamarine. Somewhat elegantly, so townspeople said.

E V E R Y O N E in town and thereabouts can tell it to you. The beginning was clear:

On the hottest day of the year in their sleeveless smocks, their glistening skins, waiting now, the third month in a row, for the delivery man to come and outfit the porch with screens, quite suddenly, all three handsome women leaned forward in their chairs and in mid-air rested their makeshift paper fans.

Coming up the road was not the screen man at all, but rather an outlander, on foot, carrying sweat stains down under the arms of his shiny tan jacket like shoulder holsters on Friday night TV. His face was obscured by the reflection off the white-hot dusty lane, but his hair when he lifted his hat to wipe his brow was dark, very dark—they all saw it clearly. It had had a proper combing with high culture grease. That was the way Maizie and **Aunt Winn** remembered it, and Mother Minto agreed.

Not until Thanksgiving did a Minto catch sight of the truck delivering screens, and by then there was no reason to greet it. The leaves were scattered over a cold ground, and already the corn was three months meditating in the county granary in Elvira. The family had other reasons for thanksgiving by then. Mr. Herman Pritikin was no longer a stranger. Out there he sat on the glass porch, which was only slightly too cold now that the upper air vents had stuck open and would not close even with a good hammering.

From the first, Herman Pritikin sat tall and stood tall both; this was something Mother Minto looked for in a man. She did not want her Maizie Lee Minto to settle with, or even sport with, a man who looked tall in his seat but who, when he stood up, turned out to be a midget with nothing between his ankles and his knees. Aunt Winn noted that Mr. Pritikin was over six feet high and well-proportioned, broad through the shoulder and not too skinny through the seat. A powerful automobile driver, Mother Minto guessed, with strong hands and thighs. When finally he took off his sunglasses, Mother Minto winced. He was like something wild and stiff on the hoof, she thought, in tan pants and pointed boots, most likely at home on land or sea.

What an Indian summer it was, so it turned out. Everywhere they swerved there was heat and in it the shadow of Herman Pritikin silent and tough. A little black pigtail hung down just slightly in the back from his neatly shaved nape; and when he got into motion, he swaggered as he went. After that, it was his mouth that captivated Mother Minto; the small pinched mouth and out of it the high voice. There was not a bit of gravel in his throat, no gruffness at all, only a whine: nasal, manly, and high. It was as if, Aunt Winn proclaimed, Mr. Pritikin spoke habitually with a plum pit clenched in his teeth and a wedding corset strangling his waist.

"That kind of lip-biting control," Maizie's mother mentioned carefully, "is one of the things we've been missing quite gladly since your father went off to the fish hatcheries."

Then they all remembered that unexpected, pinched moment when Maizie's father had sped off to the salmon canneries of Juneau, Alaska, for one unending experimental night. Yes, Mother Minto said to Aunt Winn, time had flown fast as a paper airplane through her present habitat.

"Call me, Hermes," Mr. Pritikin interjected, with a small smile on his thin lips. "They all do."

Where had they seen anything like it? mother and daughter asked in familial camaraderie. Their thighs whispered back and forth under their flannel nighties in front of the window between their twin beds. The dust of the waning summer burned slowly on the radiator under the eaves. In the moonlight, they could just make him out. Below, on the newly frosted lawn, laid out on Aunt Winn's hand-stitched, hen-and-chickens wedding quilt, Mr. Pritikin showed his boxer shorts to the stars. And there, barely visible, were the two dark spots of his chilled nipples perched like two tiny pine cones on his completely hairless chest.

Like her mother, it was as if Maizie had pretty pink peonies set into each cheek, and a figure somewhat plumpish at the top and bottom, narrow under the ribs. Maizie's laugh carried in it a lilting melody not unlike the slightly off-key tunes of the hand-bell ringers at church. Particularly it seemed to spring up, her merriment, whenever she was along or when she read—both tragedies and comedies alike. The travels of the word and the language lilting on the page were her ultimate delight—not unlike her mother who had studied the history of the worlds old and new, nor her Aunt Winn who preferred the contemplations of mathematics and the new computer rage. But always Maizie dreamed of romance—with which both mother and aunt were glad to be done.

So there he was: whistleless and uptight for the most part, tan pants tucked into boots that ran to his knees, a white cotton shirt, unbuttoned halfway down, stretched almost transparent across his broad chest. Before breakfast he showered in the only bathroom, just outside Mother Minto and Maizie Lee's room. Between the high braying of indiscernible song and the shirring of water striking strong hairless flesh, Mother Minto and daughter sat up a full fifteen minutes before the morning alarm, eyes flung open, an unmentioned flush over each of their brows. One blushed for herself, the other for her daughter and a little bit for the sake of what she called steam heat.

A dutiful guest, Herman Pritikin assumed a few chores. In the morning he took the basket with the red checkered scarf in it out to the hen house and collected the eggs.

"My goodness fat gracious," Aunt Winn said, counting out the eggs to go into town, "will you note how these hens have started to lay out."

"It's Hermes," Maizie said, rather nonchalant. "He rubs their necks."

Mother M. stopped in the dusty and feathered doorway between the packing shed and the coop.

"Yes," Maizie said, "he chucks them under the chins."

"Oh my," said Aunt Winn rubbing her throat and casting her a glance.

"Yes, and sings."

"And sings?" the two older women said together after a lifetime of silent egg gathering.

"Sings *The Yellow Rose of Texas*. And leans down to do it, too. Sings it in their earholes, right in the sides of their head."

"Oh my," Aunt Winn sighed. "Just try to extrapolate what will come next." With that the two older women looked up from the neatly filled rows of speckled brown eggs as if they had been part chicken themselves, heads jutting forward to stare though the dimly lit shack at the sleek Maizie Lee.

It was not until they all sat in the kitchen over the afternoon coffee cake that they again had a chance to speak about it. Absentmindedly, Maizie had begun to mend at a tear in the hem of her slip which she had not bothered to take off for the task. Her yellow hair swept around the sides of her intent face, swung down around the back of her shoulders like a cape, and drew in at the ribbon where she sat.

"What is it?" Maizie said, looking up from her knee with a jerk, needle in the air.

"Ask her," Aunt Winn said, bobbing her thin little face, patting the coil at the back of her head as she always did when any particular nervousness sprang up. "Ask her right now. Do it, Mother M."

"Ask me what?" Maizie Lee said, needle half in, half out of the cloth.

"Has he frisked at you yet?" Mother Minto said in a rush. "Has Mr. Hermes made an attempt?"

The needle went in and out. "Oh that—" Maizie Lee smiled. "Most certainly has."

"And?"

"It was a success."

"A success?" the two sisters cried out.

"Just this morning," she said, meeting their eyes. In the kitchen her eyes were slate blue, just as they were every day there with the white wallpaper behind her and all over it the yellow and red coffee pots thought pretty long before their own time. "Yes. This morning Herman caught hold of my wrist—I was coming out of the bathroom. He knocked the towel right off of my head. Have you ever noticed his eyes— Mama? Aunt Winn?—how beautiful they are? I was so startled, I couldn't say a word. And then, he let go of me. 'Forgive me,' he said, 'forgive me very much.' That was a frisk, wouldn't you say? Then he rushed down the stairs and into the yard."

"How very strange," the two sisters said, looking at one another most peculiarly out the adjacent corners of their own bluish-green eyes.

All day he sat on the sunporch, reading *The Practical Financier*, and calculating, he said, how to make hairpin decisions and big nerve. At supper he ate heartily and silently, staring up occasionally with his warm eyes to smile at one after the other of them. Afterward, he chose the dishtowel with the proper day of the week. Each day Aunt Winn stayed longer and longer; the two sisters had never been happier. They could not think why they had spent so much time apart while living so close for so many years. And then, no one had to say a thing. It simply was obvious: Maizie Lee, like a polished little apple, began one day to glow. And Mr. Pritikin took up whistling while he read.

"IT'S not as if they'll never do it," Mother Minto suggested, when the county neighbors came over for burnt-sugar going-away cake. As she said it, Mother Minto saw Aunt Winn meet her secret sad glance. On the far side of the living room, Maizie Lee was chatting gaily away. Yes, Mother Minto said bravely, there was not really any reason to curtsey every time you saw a stroke of good luck. Maizie herself said she was happy enough. Just then Mr. Hermes—towering over their Maizie, surrounded by guests, one hand on her arm—explained it to the county in the polished salesmanship voice he had been practicing out of books: "All in good time, dearest friends," he said, looking directly down at the top of her head and smiling quietly as if in the glossy top of her hair he could see his own face. "As you and we all of us know, in the deepest devotion of love, there is always plenty enough of it, yes. Yes, time to love, yes indeed."

And then with the backfiring of Mother Minto's old blue Chevy and a little puff of dust in the lane, the young couple was gone from the place.

N o w Aunt Winn churned up the road in her miniature truck, bringing the groceries and the news, also the letters up from the metal box that seemed large as a clothes hamper on the day of clean clothes. Mother Minto was finally after all these years somewhat content, but for the loneliness-ache in the springs of her heart where moment by moment creaked the small, recalled, growing and grown voice, from baby to woman, of her Maizie Lee.

In the late afternoons when the dinner had been put in to bake and the chores of the day had subsided, when the sheep, two cows, chickens, crops, garden and house had been tended since four thirty a.m., Mother M. sat on the porch with Aunt Winn and read and thought on the historical progress of the world up to and since the time of her degree.

As Aunt Winn in consolation said repeatedly, it was certainly an opportunity for Maizie to travel suddenly out of Wild Creek where all the short dusty roads ran at right angles and never took a curve that didn't come out just like you'd expect. By the end of one week, Maizie had already taken the whirl-i-cane view of Italy and France.

And so, but for the postcards and phone calls, for seven years, Maizie Minto dropped out of sight.

II

One day in late July a fat envelope came, complete with details, sketches, and plans. And a query for both of them. Mother Minto shook herself up out of her straw-backed rocking chair. Now she walked very slightly with a limp; time had made certain stops and alterations in the scheme of her gears. She settled down in resignation again.

"Good lordy lord," Aunt Winn said, fluttering a tissue against her chest as Mother read the circumstances again. The young couple had bought a piece of property in the desert, dirt cheap. Of all places, in the desert, in the other end of the United States.

"A curse!" Mother Minto suggested. "Is that what it is, Winny? Have we got a curly-cued gene?!"

Aunt Winn pushed her new half-glasses up on her nose, so she could look directly at the facts. "Something foul," she said.

Uncle Albert, well-remembered from their childhood and their young adult lives, too, had been shot down emotionally and financially in New Mexico during the depression by his own desert ranch. "No, Arizona."

"No," Aunt Winn said, "it was New Mexico."

"Whatever," Mother Minto said, irritably, her face turning toward red. "Whatever it was, it was west of here, and I remember his handwriting clear as if I'd written it myself. It was a 'god-forsaken place where people were *pack horses tied to a breeze,*' that's what he said. That was the first sign."

"I will never forget Mother's face," Aunt Winn said. Together they leaned over Maizie's new letter in a fret, and Aunt Winn read back the last lines of Maizie's blue-inked words again, ever so slowly.

Herman is setting up prefabricated metal shacks to sell to the retired people of America who don't have a place to lay down their weary heads. *Why not come out and move in?* The good will he is making is potent and dangerous. It sets my heart on fire every time I look at the flesh of this man.

Aunt Winn looked over the pewter frames of her new small glasses, directly into her younger sister's eyes: "Potent and dangerous?"

"After the sheath," Mother Minto said, sourly, "then comes the sword."

> P.S. I have invested seven-eighths of our three-way account toward the acquisition of a communal kitchen and facilities for the new place. Very sorry. Had no time to consult on this very good deal.

After long lip-biting silence, Mother Minto read aloud, "'Say *love* to Aunt Winn.'"

Aunt Winn rocked back on the heels of her chair. "You'll never catch me in one of those tins. As if we didn't have a place. Metal houses in the desert, imagine it." Aunt Winn pulled out the pins from the back of her hair and shoved them back in. "No matter how tired out or rotten poor we get. No matter how much of that place she says we own. We were swell-off until this."

"Who ever would have expected it? Over night, here we sit, King Tuna, part owners to the warmed-over tuna-pea casserole."

"Shake and bake is more like it. In a metal house."

With that they both looked up, and just as suddenly laughed. There they were under the same roof. They now lived together in enjoyment and good company. They took a moment to set aside the letter and deep-breathe, cursing and giving thanks for what they had in Maizie Lee—who had, since the day she was born, sometimes more indirectly than not, in one way or another, made them grateful for their lives. The same day, off went their quick reply:

> *Is there not one place in the vast southwestern desert of these United States where one photographer might not consider taking a picture of YOU, Maizie Lee Minto, as repeatedly we have begged?*

That was all they intended to say on the matter; that much

was understood. "Pritikin Village, indeed," they privately and frequently said with a shudder. A certain worry about retirement had suddenly sprung up in their financial attitudes.

Y E A R S went this way and that, maybe three or four. Corn came up in the fields and went out in the harvester. Annually there was the tallying up at Elvira, some autumns up, some autumns down. The only real change came when the hired man suddenly fell ill, and had to lie low during spring plowing time, having had several lesser parts of his body removed. For the first time since they were young brides, the two of them had the pleasure and bone-chilling weariness of riding the spring plow. And, one other thing—the sisters agreed there was not much point in so frequent a painting of the house. Now it would be white rather than blue, since it faded toward that anyway and cost an arm and a leg.

A cross-section picture postcard of layered multi-colored sand finally arrived and was tacked to the pantry wall where it stayed next to the refrigerator for two solid years.

III

In the southwestern regions of the universe, Maizie Lee Minto had turned brown as a baking powder bisquit, well done. Small horny toads lived outside her door and tumbleweeds rattled against the windows of her metal shack. So said one letter that covered sixteen months.

Other things mentioned here and there in the mail were subject repeatedly to individual or tandem recall. Several older people had joined them. A pool had been put in. And a Red Cross station with a nurse. All the staff were well-versed in CPR. Imported flowers were laid out in beds along the stone walks in imported dirt. Finally the metal shacks had come down and up went adobe huts. The metal shacks had been hauled off at not too great a loss. What a clatter the day they were lifted off the face of the desert and smashed into compacted sizes.

She had been on a vacation to Santa Fe and heard the Chamber Orchestra; then to San Francisco for the Opera. *Why does she never once consider coming home? Home is a place, isn't it?* They had put a complete stereo system in each unit. Their new business manager: "If singing to the flowers makes them grow, think how important music must be to our clients?" A small plane had been purchased with an easy runway out back. A few cacti had had to be cleared. A cactus grows higher than you might imagine—and never fails to remind me of a cartoon. *She appreciated the shorts.*

And recently, she was getting fatter. And fatter. "Do you suspect?" Aunt Winn ventured. "Might we consider—"

"How are the tomatoes?" Mother M. asked.

"Potent and dangerous," Aunt Winn laughed.

IV

Through the snow-white house in the dead middle of one ordinary night, the telephone rattled itself nearly off the wall. Together Aunt Winn and a pale Mother Minto scurried down the stairs, Aunt Winn anxiously patting back the waves of her uncoiled hair. Under the hems of their nighties their bare feet soaked up a chill that came not nearly as much from linoleum as from bad thoughts.

And then it was over, there the two of them stood, their psychologies worked up, torn into several pieces and set wildly adrift. "I heard that girl's voice," Mother Minto sobbed, sitting over a cup of emergency tea, "I recognized it after all these years clear as if it was my own—"

"Our angel crying and squawking about that traitor. We are lucky not to have been closer than six thousand miles. Or, or whatever the correct mileage is!" With that Aunt Winn picked up and set down the sugar bowl with such ferocity that the little cap on the top of the lid severed itself from the rest.

But, all in all, they were only to look back on it secretly grateful for the offshoot of all the bad news. After so many years, in less than a week, Maizie Lee Minto would be standing on the glass porch with her new little baby, Winston Churchill, in her arms. Though worn out from goings on, there would be a suntan on mother and child that couldn't have been gotten in the Wapsipinnicon Valley unless you had hired out on the back of a truck with the rest of the adolescent county punks for a blistering season to detassel corn.

I T was only a week and then they had Maizie right there for the *immense inquisition,* so the two sisters said to her beautiful actual face, laughing lightly and brightly in their flowered bib-aprons as they put up autumn pears. There was their own Winston Churchill, a sweet, pie-faced baby child with stout normal legs and black hair, and a mouth broad and healthy like his mother's.

"And a whalloping good thing that mouth is," Mother Minto exclaimed, tickling his lip until he sucked one finger at the tip. There was no need to mention the tight rubber mouth of Mr. Hermes which the two older women had imagined closing in, nightly, on Maizie Lee. They had already talked about that for seven days running. To their further relief Maizie Lee had named Winny not for any of Hermes' family. She had named him, she said, for dignity in times of distress and for her aunt who had cared so lovingly for her dear mother while she had been away.

The steam rose off the kettle. Maizie's hair was harnessed back in a bouncing yellow tail as she pushed up her bangs with her forearm, blowing and contorting her mouth. The straight stalks of her bangs set to rustling on her head as she spoke:

She had, though heart-mashed and broken, gained several good things from what she now saw had been her first and last foray from the certainties of home. Most important, she had gotten her own little Winston, who though occasionally dour, was a sweet boy who doted on her and could be seen already to be smart. No, Maizie Lee had not been completely fool-hardy in love.

For another instance: she, Maizie Lee Minto, had never once given up her moneys to her mate; the only joint banking account she had ever shared was the one with her mother and aunt in Wild Creek. Investment, yes. But that was hardly the same thing.

"But you said seven-eighths—"

"An investment," Maizie smiled. "We got it all back. All of it."

"You kept your own money?" Mother M. asked, passing over other concerns, incredulous. "Your own? You kept it yourself?"

"A strict half of all profits and expenses, that's what I got. To the penny. Of course, I had to pay rent."

"You had to pay rent in your own house?"

"Rent?" Aunt Winn exclaimed. "He made you pay rent?"

"Yes," Maizie Lee said. "But he cannot legally touch my banking account."

Aunt Winn sat down with a start. "This is a moment of sudden learning," Aunt Winn said in dismay and delight.

"But how did you find out? About him?" Mother Minto asked a little too loudly, leaning up against the counter, as if communing with the next pile of ripe yellow fruit. "About his—infidelity?"

At that, Maizie Lee laid the big knife into the chopping of thick yellow pears while Aunt Winn began to core and Mother Minto skinned their covers away.

Then, just as suddenly, Maizie's knife stopped and then the other two. "First, it was all those inexplicable damned trips," Maizie said hoarsely. Mother M. laid her clean hand on her arm, and Aunt Winn moved beside her. "And then it was a picture I found in his bottom dresser drawer."

The sisters stood back for a second, aghast, and then moved closer again. Aunt Winn rubbed at her shoulder with one hand. "Not a picture. How cruel."

"It was of an older man—" Maizie said to them.

"An older *man!*"

"Yes," Maizie said.

"A man?"

"Oh, well—" Aunt Winn hastily offered. "Of course, it's not our own way to do; but, Maizie—"

"You see, the picture showed an older man—who looked a *lot* like Herman!—in prison stripes up against a stone wall."

"That is more than even I can acknowledge," Aunt Winn exhaled. "Your man went in for it before the camera! with an imprisoned man! in uniform!—up against a stone wall!"

And then all they could get out of her, leaning against the cabinet that way, laughing and sobbing, for a minute or two, even with a cup of ice-lemonade was, "I'm so glad to be home."

"Dearest baby—" Mother Minto stroked the sweat from underneath the little blonde sticks of her bangs. "If I had known such depravity would lurch after you, Sweetness, I'd have shot that man off our property the second he lifted his glassy-eyed face."

Mother Minto lifted her fist to the sky. "To think that that man—don't say his name!—your husband that was and was not, the father of our own little Winston Churchill, was stepping out—with a convict who was escaped, and even worse! Eventually killed by the state."

"Not the firing squad!" Aunt Winn breathed. On the far side of the kitchen, Winston Churchill played happily in his net pen. "Poor Winny," Aunt Winn crowed in disbelief.

Maizie Lee set down the jar of cinnamon sticks and then she sat down in one of the kitchen straight back chairs with the flat maple seats and laughed until she cried. "No no, it wasn't like that at all. The picture was of Herman's *grandfather.*"

The air smelled of the love of pungent steamed pears. "With his grandfather?"

"Mama! Auntie Winn!" Maizie choked, but then she was bent over her knees and they could not tell whether it was a laugh or a howl of pain. Together they crouched down before her and pulled her brown hands from her face. She was laughing so hard she could not speak, and the tears thundered down her cheeks.

"There now," Aunt Winn said, rushing for the dipper to bring her some water. "There now, sip this. Try to relax. We won't say another word, neither of us."

Together they held to her hands while she got hold of herself. Then they watched her drinking slowly at first and then greedily, taking in the familiar, good iron bite of the cold wellwater going down.

"All right now—" she said, squeezing their hands. "Let's get it straight." She bounced their hands up and down on her knees. She squeezed their hands again. "Straight is quite bad enough, but not what you think. Here's what happened, the whole story that I later found out. You see, Herman's grandfather was arrested long before Herman was born, when the grandfather was fairly young. For bigamy. Herman saved the picture all those years, but when I asked him, he was *embarrassed* about it in a way I couldn't explain. You asked how I found out. That was one of the clues."

"A grand-daddy for a bigamist—" Aunt Winn sighed miserably. She leaned back and drew up a chair to set her yet birdlike figure down in dismay. She had grown slightly stocky about the frame with her thin legs still poking out as if from the ruff. Across the room, Mother Minto crept open the window to the pantry to let in a little breeze. "Sit down, Mother M.," Aunt Winn said again, "before you faint dead away." So then there they all sat in a powwow, the three of them in the middle of the vast open space of their own kitchen floor, chair to chair.

"That's right," Maizie Lee sighed.

Angrily, Aunt Winn drummed the underside of her chair.

"That tight-pantsed bounder had it crawling in his veins—like parasites," Mother Minto said bitterly.

"Think of it! To inherit bigamy. And then not even to manage to marry it once."

With that, the round Winston let out a shrill scream.

"No no, not you, darling," the two older women fluttered, staring at him as if he was only just newly born. "Of course not! You're nothing like him at all. Eat your cookie, sweet pea," they cried almost in unison. Aunt Winn put an elephant-shaped cracker in his roly-poly hand and directed it toward his mouth. "I can't believe how good he's been, and for so long."

"He's always like that," Maizie said, staring proudly at him.

"Go on, Maizie Lee," Mother Minto said. "We will steel ourselves for the rest."

"He was gone so much while I was pregnant—that he made me nervous more and more. I was going to call you but first I thought I'd wait and see if it would take, and then I thought everything was falling apart."

"There now," Aunt Winn said. "You don't need to explain. We can see perfectly well."

"Finally I asked him: 'What are you doing?' I said. He was looking after our investments, that's what he said. After Winnie was born, I found another set of baby clothes in the back of his closet. The only thing was—" Maizie said with a catch in her voice, "they were just like the exact ones Winnie had on."

As if two good apple jack bottles had been freshly uncorked, the two jaws dropped and set. "Not just another woman?" Aunt Winn squeaked.

"They were born the same month."

"And to think—" Mother Minto said, after everyone had calmed. It was still twenty minutes until the pear jam would be cooked down. In a fury she kicked off her shoes and thrust her feet onto the sill against the new screens. "And to think he never married either one, not you or that other poor girl. She got caught up just the same—swept halfway around the world like a toy boat."

"That's right," Maizie sighed. "And what a surprise—come to find out there were other passengers on board."

Aunt Winn tssked for some time, and Mother M. sat in silence tapping her right toe against the screen, considering the juncture of inside and out. And then they all gazed fondly as the little Winston Churchill buzzed sweetly at his mother's breast. Soon enough, Aunt Winn pulled her watch out of the bib of her long apron. "Time to ladle up."

Just as they got to the kitchen and Mother Minto made to stick the ladle in and spoon the sauce into all the clean-boiled jars, Aunt Winn held up her hand. From the bottle over the sink, Aunt Winn fetched out a new cinnamon stick they had bought that week from the all-purpose store. "Time to take the taste of that vile story out of this jam," she said.

"It's a modernist curse," Mother M. said, "the likes of which we have not seen since the Roman world."

And so they each took a lick and then Aunt Winn threw the stick into the pot for a quick stir. "And now, Mother M.," Aunt Winn said, "we are ready to pour."

V

The day Winston turned three and surpassed his terrible contrary year, Aunt Winn looked out the frosted glass of the porch from over her early winter knitting and cried out in a muffled, uncharacteristic squeal. Maizie Lee and Mother M. heard it even upstairs where they had their heads stuck in a stack of new-dyed wool and moth treatment balls. Perhaps something had happened to Winston, they thought, who loved to play with Aunt Winn's yarn, winding and unwinding it carefully at her feet.

In a matter of seconds all three women stood on the porch staring at the vision of horror on the crystalized glittering new lane of snow. A fur-coated, large figure with a floppy fur hat riding over the darkest of glasses was striding up their lane in tall tan leather boots; and behind him, like a sign, was a trail of double deep prints like smoke cast out from a dual exhaust.

Aunt Winn picked up Winston Churchill and clutched him to her chest. "Do not," Aunt Winn said, "let that murderer into this house."

Through the glass pane of the back door, they stared at the snowflakes stuck like stars onto the furry tips of his hat, his sunglasses still attached firmly to his face, the yammering up and down of his strong jaw. His leather glove tapped relentlessly at one spot on the door.

"Don't do it."

Fast as iron filings, Maizie Lee's hand shot toward the latch, just as he, her Hermes, lifted up the sunglasses and, through the frost patterns of the window, showed his electronic eyes.

On the sunporch he put his black and red argyle socks up on the coffee table and sipped at his tea. With such grace and candor he presented his story to them. He had come on business, he said. "On the business of love without regret."

Maizie Lee sat on the sofa between her mother and aunt, the three of them laced elbow to arm, Winston held tightly on her lap.

He had invested all his savings in a deal he thought she might wish to understand. "I am certain," he said gaily, "that you will be thrilled to the toes. Maizie love, I have had the foresight to take a written liberty with your name."

"Oil?" the group of them cried in disdain.

"What do you mean, 'in oil'?" Mother M. said nastily.

"Yes," he said. "A new company, brand spanking new!" He took out a brown cigarette, fixed it into his mahogany holder, and filled the room with a dark cloud. "I have been given just one chance in a lifetime, and this is it," intoned his highest, strong voice. His eyes blazed into Maizie Lee's. "How could I fail to share such good fortune with the honeybee of my dreams?"

Aunt Winn plumped herself up, a mad partridge on the couch, vindictive and alert. "What do you mean—a new company? A subsidiary or some such whirlimagig? Make yourself clear. You have no legal share to her name, not her money or her name!"

"Not so!" Herman declared. "Seek innocence and you shall find strength." And then he explained.

"They've not even drilled!" Maizie Lee yelled. "You forged my name, with all my mother's savings and Aunt Winn's, too, for a not-even-drilled?"

"My godfrey daniels," Aunt Winn breathed.

"Don't do it," Mother Minto said.

"He's already done it, Mother," Maizie Lee snapped. "He's signed my name."

"There are courts, there are laws—" one of the women said.

"That is absolutely correct, my three graces," Mr. Hermes said. "There's nothing *not* to do. Just sit back and reap." Herman Pritikin slid his hand down his new red tie with the wide yellow squiggles swimming on it. "I've acted on your joint behalfs. A court case would cost you a mint."

It was as if everyone sitting on the sofa had wilted in a late summer heat. Maizie Lee would never take to court the father of her boy—for little Winston's sake; they knew that much, each of them. For fear she would lose him to his father's custody, to the man with the slick silver tongue.

W H E N finally Mr. Hermes had eaten the last of the pear jelly, and also the plum jam they had set up for winter, he roused himself from the glass porch where he had been sleeping each night in his fur coat and set out to seek their fortunes. Stiffly they stood, as he fixed his sunglasses onto his nose and stampeded himself down the muddy spring road. It had taken an act of God to keep her from sleeping with him, Maizie Lee confessed to her mother and aunt. Each night with the bedroom door locked she had slept on her back with the little sleeping Winston humming peacefully and tied carefully with a dish towel onto her chest while Hermes, just outside, kept up his late vigil, tapping incessantly on the upper third of the door with his gold-plated ring.

VI

Summer fled past in a flurry of worries and conjectures and recitations of how it had been all winter in the company of the likes of Mr. Hermes again. Come late August, the hired man got in a good crop of soybeans and corn—all to go into a new account at the bank in Wild Creek. The evening temperatures plummeted further each night, and it seemed as if they might all forget about him. The three women and Winston were looking forward to a quiet autumn enlivened only by hot turkey celebrations and the caring for the animals and plants of their farm, to the housecleaning and sewing, pie making and pie eating, when the phone rang again. From somewhere south a call was coming in.

Aunt Winn went to get it. After a moment she came into the sitting porch. "I wouldn't pick up if I were you," she said directly to Maizie. "It's that character in the fur bonnet—you know who—with the two glass circles for eyes."

"On the other hand," Mother Minto said from the couch, "the wretch has our savings at stake."

"Money is nothing," Aunt Winn declared. "We have each other, we're happy and together. Give the monster the breeze."

In the kitchen Maizie Lee stuck the receiver in amongst her shoulder-length, newly curled blonde hair, and just as quickly they all leaned together to hear him say: "I'm a changed man. And you, Maizie Lee, were my first extraordinary thought. I'm a new person, Maizie Lee. It was like an operation on the mind."

"Whatever do you mean?" Maizie Lee asked with a distinct element of ice wrapped around her voice. "Where are you anyway?"

"I am here in myself, where I am always at home. Temporarily I'm in Nashville. And what have I done? I have enrolled in a program and completed the course in two days. You see before you a changed man."

"But what have you changed?" Maizie Lee asked with no small amount of exasperation in her voice.

"Why, sweetness," he said, his voice ecstatic, nearly a squeak. "I have done the inevitable. I have been *actualized*."

Mother Minto shook her head over the receiver next to Aunt Winn.

And what he had found, he went on, Maizie Lee would not

believe. He was not only actualized, he confessed, but he was in love. "Come to me, Maizie Lee," he cried out across the miles. "Come home to Daddy Hermes. Make me love you as much as I now love myself." Together they all looked into the mouthpiece of the phone as if they could see him there in the one dark lenslike cap with all the holes running through it. There were tears—actual tears, everyone heard them—in his voice.

And what about the money? the two older women asked when the phone was hanging on its hook. They had forgotten to ask.

T H E week Maizie Lee went to be actualized was the hardest time of Aunt Winn and Mother Minto's life. Each day they looked onto the little limbs of young Winston Churchill, into his round chirping face, onto the small lump of his covers while he slept, onto his breakfast things spattered with cereal and spilled juice, and wept. What if he or the two of them took him away? And Maizie Lee gone again, too. The telephone did not ring until the end of the interminable time.

"The ceremony," Maizie Lee shouted over the wires, "was a terrific success!"

The two women fell together over the telephone, like two pencils in a cup. "The ceremony?!"

"The actualization!" the crackly voice of Maizie Lee came back. Yesterday had been the culmination of a week of excruciating classes for her. During the first twenty-four hours she had been confined with people who spoke to her only in southern and eastern dialects. She was not allowed to eat or drink anything, not even water; and she confessed, not any of the actualees had been to the facilities once.

"In the music capitol of the world? At a big conference like that?" Mother Minto shook her head and wept. Little Winston's face pressed against his grandmother's thigh as she stroked the top of his head.

Maizie Lee's changed voice cracked through the phone like
a young boy's. "I survived! And Herman was right there all
the time, helping me through. Finally I know who I am!"

The two grown women looked at one another and then
into the phone, and said together in one high terrified voice:
"Who? Who are you, Maizie Lee?"

But the telephone crackled just then and they could not
quite understand. "What was it?" they called out again.

"It's like in the *Wizard of Oz* at the end—" came Maizie
Lee's voice.

"Yes?" the two older women asked; it was a movie neither
had liked. "Come on home now," Aunt Winn consoled deli-
cately. "I do expect, after all that, that you feel struck in the
head."

"Yes," Mother implored, "you'll come home and leave that
bad man behind."

"No no, he's not a bad man," Maizie chirped. "No, he's not a
bad man: there are no bad men," she said. "He's just, well—"

"What's that?" The two women gasped. "What did you
say?"

"He's just not for me."

As if caught up on the first giddy breeze of the balmiest
spring, the two older women sighed. Mother M. and Aunt
Winn burst simultaneously into fresh tears.

"And Winston?" They pressed him tightly between
themselves.

"For the rest of our lives, Hermes and I will sever our relationship, leave it as friends who love but no longer speak."

A rumble of high pitched conversation overtook the background, not static, not sense. Mother M. could not make it
out. It sounded very much like a flock of birds on a migratory
flight.

"But what about Winny?" Mother M. shouted with a touch
of anger in her voice. "Will what's-his-name have rights? Will
he take Winny away?"

"Why, Mother, Winston will remain just as he is. With us, of
course."

"Yes!" A leaping of women and infants.

"And one other thing!" Maizie Lee said with emphasis.

A silence of dread.

"You'll never guess in all of your lives—"

"What is it!" they cried. "You come home this instant and don't do anything else, do you hear?"

"That company? That new one, you know—"

"We know very well which one," Aunt Winn said fiercely.

"They struck oil. Auntie Winn, Mama, can you believe it?"

"The company with our money?"

"Banana oil, that's what he struck," put in Aunt Winn.

"Yes," Maizie Lee laughed, high and clear like a glass bell. "I mean no. He struck oil. Actual oil." They could almost see her newly curled pony tail swinging. "He struck it rich for all of us—that other poor woman, too!"

VII

And so it was determined, as the story was discussed over the years and compared with similar county happenings, that it was not necessarily true that all good luck must run to bad, that what had happened to Mother Minto must happen just the same to her daughter, nor—following upon the same line of reasoning—would it be necessary that little Winston would grow up to be a leaper and a bounder. So Aunt Winn decided one day, and Mother Minto agreed. There were similarities, that much was true. But progress could be made if you looked to your head.

Upon one other thing they conferred and concluded: there were only so many chances in life, and they had taken more than their share over Mr. Hermes, that was for sure. That phase was over, never again to be reentered for fear of false returns. Mr. Hermes was informed by a lawyer of this in kindly strong words. Mother and aunt granted themselves permission to take firm steps—to this Maizie Lee Minto gave her own strong assent. They would tie Maizie up, completely out of sight, if ever Mr. Hermes came tapping again.

Three of them, Aunt Winn, Mother Minto, and the young
Winston Churchill in his junior-size jeans and tiny Brooks
Brothers' shirt, set out for the town of Wild Creek on the same
day Maizie Lee set off on the school bus to her new job teaching foreign languages at the county school.

The dust flew out from under their newest blue acquisition;
in streamed the sun through side windows and vents,
through the pollinating corn's golden mist. And then to please
their young Winston, the new sunroof was peeled back. "My
oh my," Aunt Winn said, as the incoming breeze lifted their
hair, "isn't it as if a glory had settled in our own heads?"

"Don't you just feel it?" Mother M. exclaimed. "Everything
here is right with the world, everything is just the way it most
ought to be." In the back, in his carseat, Winnie crowed along,
singing along with the rear speakers. Down the county strip of
gravel and dried mud they sped, along the Wapsapinnicon
County road that severed Wild Creek corn and soybeans and
sheep from Elvira's alfalfa and cows. The upholstered leather
glowed like butter, as here, then there, they churned past the
reds and oranges of their neighbor's farms. Chickens fluttered
by like white carnations in the yards.

In town they ordered up as surprises for Maizie, in celebration of her return and the beginning of her new and actual
life: Proust's *Remembrance of Things Past* in the original French
as Mother Minto said, "to satiate the insatiate"; one top-of-
the line Caterpillar tractor with an enclosed air-conditioned
cab; the new Modern Library edition of Gibbon's *Decline and
Fall*; a spanking new henhouse with individual roosting com-
partments and a pair of fancy feather-footed Dutch fowl;
ninety-five gallons of paint sky-blue; six mid-calf length
dresses and beautiful jackets, a pair of gray leather boots,
fourteen silk blouses, and three pairs of new jeans; a full-
length resilvered mirror; six hundred prime Elvira acres and a
herd of top Guernsey cows complete with ranch help and a
veritable tree of milking machines; one library card, local,
with access to the interstate traveling book bus; one new-
fangled home entertainment center complete with music and

films; a paid-up subscription to Madrigals of the Month; for the sun porch, quadruple-pane glass with wind-out convertible screens in mahogany frames; a new furnace and central air for the rest of the house; a greenhouse, sauna, and sunken bath with revolving whirlpool jets; one outdoor swimming pool with two-meter board to drive off summer heat; an antique roll-top desk with built-in graphical computer and life-time paper, ribbons, and pens; a set of floral print curtains and sheets for her new canopy bed; and in case she should feel selfish or receive no mail of importance, sixteen substantial contributions in her name to national and local charity groups; an immense savings bond for Winston Churchill; and, little Winston's idea, three horses and a pony, and four two-wheeled bikes; a dishwasher soon to be built in; one mail-order fertile peacock and its mate, Aunt Winn's life-long dream; a kit for a twenty-foot backyard gazebo, with screens; and—from the Wild Creek Asylum and Infirmary—a stiff white straightjacket with reinforced straps, as Aunt Winn put it: should all this fail and there ever be an urgent need.

*S*oundings in Feet and Fathoms

White Water

A N D my Alex refuses to speak to me for close onto a week until I pry it out of him with a walk in the woods and a lot of quizzes and sullen replies. Finally, he says, why'd you let him die? The child not in his class at all but every grade of the school children have taken a first hurt from it and the story goes around that the father of Alex Adams, who has turned to the special mechanics of doctoring, has let the child go—out of error, or malevolence.

School children passing the word around: I, Robert Adams, M.D., Doctor of Misery, let the kid die. The first one they have known to die in their school. A sweet child. Mostly unknown at the school. Shy. Let him die. And the parents cannot admit as to what was the truth. Living it day to day now. The mistake of their century. Too unbelievable even for me. So I told him straight out how it was. How the parents in the corner house in town with the big wide unobtrusive New England porch and apple tree where Alex has never played let down their own son. Schoolchildren tormenting Alex over it every day now; these things we do not speak of to our friends. Perhaps a gross mistake; only so much one can divulge. And it is spring and all these thoughts come sailing in. The dogs are baying up and down the valley. I will not consider what it is that they are looking for. Dogs.

I laid my hands on my son's head and I said to him: The way it was. The little boy's own papa backed out of the drive and ran over him. His mama was in the car. Going hysterical like most any parent would standing on the funereal borders of his/her child's life—even without the guilt of the accident, the thump beneath the wheel, they are crying out: Whidby! Whidby! Please call Dr. Whidby, please. And old Whidby is at that very same moment deep perhaps in a dream of marmalade or some such other sweet thing—twenty-five miles away. A silence most profound fallen over the waiting room when that is explained in no uncertain terms. Whidby would have called me in, your own father, Alexei, even if Whidby had been available and in the range of call. Heads not Whidby's arena. Whidby a man of the heart. And the two parents of the first grader, made minuscule god down at the Eisenhower Elementary School, have gone completely paralyzed with the moment and what should emerge but something unpredictable, something so staid and meant to stop this motion that will carry their son away into a land very much unknown: Whidby must come! they cry. You cannot operate! You cannot! The woman holding to the shaking arm of her husband, most unfortunate driver of automobiles. All precautions of explanation and experience and logistics explained by myself: the cap of the soul lifted off most tenderly and the shrapnel of the tragedy to be removed. A hundred times I have done the deed successfully without impairment. Life and treasured limbs. A classic case with extreme urgency, I say. Prognosis fair to good. We have but few moments here for discussion, I say with a restraint I do not know from where it comes. And they are looking at me with a fear that goes even beyond the extent we see here in this calamity. A look of horror I have not seen much of since before the last big march. Look of hate by way of skin. I am growing most angry then. Mrs. O. must jump into her white pointed cap with the double black bar on the rim and give them the word, explain the necessities I have just explained. Necessity of speed. Skull fracture, I must put it to them again, soft as a cat's paw by way of encouragement toward haste. Subdural hemorrhage, decreasing respiration and rising blood pressure, spinal fluid in the nose and ears.

Mrs. O. comes back behind the sheet with a sweat across her brow and looks toward me, she cannot look at the little towhead where we have already shaved his curls away and the orderlies ready to put the kid on wheels and roll him in under the lights. She shakes her head. They will not sign. I am slow to get onto the story. She says it, finally: Whidby their man, most white.

Two prime time little thin-necktied twits looking just the same while their thin-limbed son with the scrape and bandaid star on one knee is raging with a catastrophe that makes him see the stars of the almighty king. And I said: No one, man, is coming down here quick enough to save your child, your little baby is going to die if you go on with this cause I can't cut lessen you say *cut* and you are gonna drive it this far, aren't you. I laid it onto the father: You're gonna kill this child twice, is that what you say? Let's just be sane. All human beings are born with some intelligence. I am the best for these things in most parts, and your boy is needing the best. Back there behind that curtain, his little soul is about to flutter away because you are so slow in giving the go-ahead.

And Mrs. O. with the blue hair almost ready for her retirement, must say to them once again—You don't understand, he's telling you the truth! He's the very best. No one will come out here fast enough. It's the truth, it's the truth: your baby is going to die. That little boy in there!

The two of them stood there side by side like that Segantini watercolor. Just two bumps on the side of a hill waiting for their baby to go under for love of good white hands to lay his cranium in. Good white hands of his Daddy Jesus who underwent yet another bleach job of history somewheres around the

First World War. And the kid not much less the age of Alex and no more. And there was in my mind a bad case, I told my Alexei, of the anxieties as I see them frozen in their murderous convictions of we/they and determined to carry it through to the living/dead. And I am in the turnarounds looking from them to the sheet that hangs between me and the little white brow that is yet sweet and irresponsible. No. I would not take it onto myself. I would not rescue the little innocent towhead out of the hands of his parents who would kill him so as not to be sullied by the hands of the black man. I would not set myself up to be sued by his parents and never again be able to save another towhead or let another one go more lightly than might some other heavy-handed, thick-tongued barbarian of a doctor who has nothing to say when the verdict is *no* except *get out*. And I will not risk my own children, I said, and as far as I have come to get them out from all of that.

So I said to them and so I repeated it to Alex so that he would know that it is with you no matter how or where you rise. It is a shirt you wear on your bones from before you are given the breath and until long after the breath is taken away. They wouldn't let me cut and I said to them—Wheel your white fish out, you motherfuckers. Your dead white fish was just a sorrowful kid who wanted to stay up late like all the other kids, who saw instead the daylight break right over his head because you made him into white bread instead of saying he was yours when he needed you. You made him die, your son. Take your dead white fish home that was your boy and stick him in the ground. Soon he's gonna stink almost as bad as you, two dead white fish with the superficial intelligence. And they stand there like tombs of themselves.

I sprang up myself, I said, from the pits of mediocrity! And a bigotry rotting like a worm somewheres between my liver and my spleen. What happened to you? I said. I suppose you got nothing but ignorance for your excuse, murderers. That's your own fault, I said. Whoa now, I said to myself. Whoa. I want to take an axe to their skulls if they won't let me cut on that baby who has nothing but the sound of his father's stertorous bigotry nudging his sine waves toward a flatness from which there is no—count 'em—no return.

And so I refused my own will that day. I turned the other cheek. I said: Slap me again, but I will not lift a hand. I will not go up against the law. And they rolled him out to the morgue within the hour and old Whidby would not come out of his bed as he knew they already had the best and what the fuck were they doing getting him out when they had me? If you ask this one, I say, it was no betrayal at all from white man to white man as the thin neckties kept singing out. Why should Whidby participate in such low comedy? He had my word the kid would be gone by the time he got his door light on and his car backed out into the drive. And it was the truth. I have never been much on perfecting the nature of the lie; that has seemed always to me a self-desecration I myself could easily do without, being desecrated in this life enough for one man.

W. H. Whidby gave those thin neckties in whiteface the best advice he could. He told it to Mrs. O. the way he always did, raw and straight from the mouth, intending as always the translations of the prim Mrs. O., the careful phraseology of the concerned and perfectly tender, perfectly proper and genteel: "Shut the fuck up about your superstitions," W. H. said to our Emily O. to tell them. But Mrs. O. for the first time in her life quoted him exactly. Words Mrs. O. could not have constructed for her life: "'Go back to the sticks where you were raised and bury your son among white folks if that's your pleasure in the matter, but don't bother me.'"

"Fucking bigots," he said further to the blue-haired secretary personally. And she nods to me and shakes her head. And Mrs. O. hands me the other phone, I am that shaken, and puts her finger to her mouth. Together we listen to W. H. Whidby.

"We are nothing but positive and negative bits in a magneto, Emily. Don't cry about this one, Em," he said. "This is a bad one. Can you discern it? Tell the low-lifes what I said, and give Dr. Adams a little extra cream in his tea." And so the kid died and it was as simple as one-potato-two.

Breach

Don't push! It was a breach. And I slapped her on the back; we were taking in the breaths together like one lung, but for her it was pain. They will put it to you that you can know how it is, but that is a lie. Nobody else can know your own disease, or pain, or even your fructuousness. No one body can know; it is only the dreamer's belief. If anybody knew it to be like Marie knew it, I came close at least. To be a lung is not to be, it is only an hypothesis. Our second child came out of her—the little whelp—and was beautiful, slippery as a puppy or a seal and curled up like a bell. She was a bell and we gave her the name. The nurse dropped her on the bloated belly of Marie and Marie said—Sam. Sammy, so that she could on paper be treated the same as anybody if she chose. And the name itself is to remind her where she's been and is. And everybody is looking between her legs. And Marie, too, is staring at the mirror and shouting with me to see the infant cunt inside the mother cunt like the inside of a chestnut wrinkled up and bisected but brown and laid into a bigger one. I have not seen anything more beautiful—not one thing but one that comes close and that one being a glass reproduction of one bough of the *Camellia sinensis* with its magnified sexual plant parts made of glass so beautiful that Marie and Leslie Bailey and I leaned over the exhibition case and nearly snuffed the fragrance of southern Asia from that botanical module it looked so real. And I said to myself so this is the University where anything can be done to look like the real when even it is not. They got themselves a fake plantation of obscure plants and parts here. Alexander's name acquired the same. *Camellia sinensis* we nearly called our Sammy till we thought up the difference between fake and real in the emulation of the source, the would-be namesake having had its genesis in the crafted replica of lovely, fragile tea. And if we had thought of it that way around, tea first, it might have stuck. Camala, a close second. But Sammy was her name.

H o w glorious the light now, these trees! Four hundred years old or more. The road, too, and the houses. The cubic sheds that attach to the barns. The white meadow steadying itself for acid rain. The birches white against white, a tangle of wire in the light. Trees take upon themselves their own forms, and then the fence posts and the blue-white crests of snow.

A Hound of Rock

Baying up and down the valley: bloodhounds. We will not peruse the thought of that now. Always the worrying precedes the good news. I myself have traversed half the county by my own foot looking for him. Up and down Old North Road, through my woods, and alongside the isolated lake where the early spring shore turns abruptly from the rock to the sand; that is where Alex likes to take Edward, the imaginary friend. "We dipped, Pops, in the lake, we dangled from the cliff."

"We?"

"Me and Edward."

"Edwardo and I. That would be Edwardo the ghost?"

"He's not a ghost, Daddy!"

"Were you and Edwardo in the positive sure your rope would hold that tire tight? Might be one nasty surprise there, Alex, to find yourself stuck in that tire and plummeting like a rock."

His little glasses tilt up like I am the first human answer to life on earth. "Edward checked," he said.

"You be checking that thing yourself, Alexander. You hear me now? You be checking out your own safety wherever you are finding yourself. Do you hear what I am saying at you, now Alex? Do you hear what I say?"

I am looking out onto my own back yard, the privacy of my dock unhindered by the comings, the goings of anyone at all, and I am saying to myself this is not Haight Ashbury. This is not Harlem where I found myself to be started up and grown.

If by nightfall they have not found him, the hills will be the fireflies of search beams, rising and falling. If they do not find him tonight, then tomorrow. They will drag the lake. And where is my boy?

On the scent of a small green t-shirt, green of June grass, on the scent of a kangaroo leaping on the back, now go the dogs and the county police. Now go Marie and Leslie Bailey with Carlisle shouting for him in town. *This is not my sister with the scour powder scrubbing steps to someone else's porch.* Even yet, even here in what I have known, been next to twenty years now, I am not easy with it. Where is my boy? Number for number, I am the freak of my clan and their hope. Come Sunday afternoons I am down at the clinic for the homeless where I look myself—black yellow brown white red and gray—in the face. Where is my son? I am fallible, too. I am a man. Q.E.D.

Herds down at the school tormenting Alexei most every day of his life and partly for something they think I have done. Wish to think.

He is littler than they, smarter than they, blacker than the finest ace. Wears the glasses that mark him the brain. This man, your father, was once the man of the revolution, scared shit out of them. Whoa now, they say, when they look up from their corn flakes to see that your daddy, Alex, a black man has out and out settled in the throne of their mysterious acknowledgment. It is the vitriol of ambivalence we see here flying around. And Alex already is biting it. If he is a man when he grows up he will feel it till they put him into the ground. Nada Quiddity.

Once I stood on the steps of academe, apparati of the media running all over the place. See these, I thought, your insulated wires, let them be jumper cables to the entire world of color. Then my friend C.C. claps his hand onto my back just as it is my time to give them the rap. And I have to say to myself: ain't no easy congregation, ain't no simple way. Still I am carrying a suspicious bone. A qualified anatomist is unlikely to find it, pathologist just as hopeless in the task. The bone I am talking

about is not the bone of love. Bone of contention I am worrying.

push/
    dontpush

*And now a question: Can we say that the blizzard is steadily permeat-
ing those insular arcs of acrid light under every street lamp?*
   Be taking my Alex next to one hundred fifty years to recover
from the chastisement they are giving him every recess, lunch
hour, post-school and pre-school and during class as well.
They are like a team of flying bombardier gnats and mud flies.
Every day since the incident of his little schoolmate, he comes
home with his stocking hat ripped and his soul stomped halfway into the ground. Not to mention a serious bruising too
regular to bear thought. I myself as a child had it very much
the same. Edwardo is his new friend. What color is your Edwardo there, Alexei? I say to my son out of curiosity. Alexei
stares at his father: Daddy, can't you see? Edward hasn't *got* a
color, Daddy. Can't you see?
   Alex, the only black son in his class. Sweetly we rock tied to
the dock by not much more than a string.

Night Voyages

   ". . . a huge gash in the wall with fat cells hanging off it . . .
blood came in so fast that the aperture split—whoa!—ver-
tically and laterally at the one same damn moment. We were
whizzing around so fast on that raft I would not have noticed
my own fat sweet Marie standing off there in the valve. And
then—it was down the pipe. Get your brain around this one:
when we landed we were digging with picks and shovels,
man—for clams! For simple fucking quahogs, man, in full op-
erating-room regalia: masks, booties, duds, everything.
Wieee-ew! I said to myself in that dream, wieee-zowie!, that
was one rough s.o.b. of a reverie—made it through all right

though. That's what I was thinking on that beach. Here we are on this Easter Island, see. Get that? That's where we ran the raft aground—amid headless human trunks and trunkless human heads carved out of stones.

"So I snatched up a big one, slugged the clam up against a rock. Lunchtime, I thought. About time, too. *Open, sesame!* And there flapped out a human mouth. You might just know—The son of a bitch was retching, heaving up blood faster than the tide could take it away.

"I've only had the little reverie one night a week now, every week . . ."

Plumb Bob

And it ain't going nowhere, Alexei. It isn't even new. Not six hours ago, Alex, I stood at the back of the house and was hearing a sound, not a word, not whine nor yelp, not even a note coming at me from the lake. And I knew it was you, found, though it was a sound being unintelligible by any usual means. Once I was rushing toward the lake toward you and I did not even see, though I felt them through the reassurance of something I have made with my wife: aspects of home. Felt the hard jolt as my feet hit every once in a great while the ground rapidly tilting away. Every once in a while I gave the ground a good kick. Sure that you were saved.

Your Dostoevski he felt it when they stood him within breath of the executioner's orifice, only then to hear in a whisper that it was exile not death that he got. Only the hand of God—and the fact he had not already hung himself in despair of the world—snatched him up and set him down in Siberia, not a pleasant place. Left him his sweet disillusionment to torment him the rest of his life. Disillusionment, Alex, is the sure-fired salve of the individual mind. How it does burn while it heals, little man.

Alexei, I say this: Learning to read a person is like onto reading a book; but most parts of the world do not know this; they are being too lazy to look more than once or read the fine print.

There are persons who make up whole lives of first sight and coincidence, who have wisdom called naught. Nada Quiddity, your mama says, when we have once again and hereafter encountered such a case of the We/Theys. Bring on the Nada Quidam! she calls out as if our assailants were pom-poms on a stage. She is the upright and substantial of my life. You got to know when to push and when to tuck in.

There are many ways to kill a person. Some say a life is a body, some say a spirit, some are saying both or in between. No matter how you put it, when something is snuffed seriously it is dead. The willful propagation of the misunderstandings among peoples, the perpetration of confusion, neglect, silent consent, the insidious lie, the deception and self-interest that lead to hunger and cold and the failure to thrive, that lead to the failure of the human will to love and learn is the killing of a whole people anytime it occurs to any little child no matter how old he/she is. This I am saying to you, Alexei. You may make yourself a friend out of an image, but don't you ever, Alexei, make an image out of any part of human kind and that is including yourself. And I am not talking here, Alex, of the superficial image, the photograph, the television screen. I am talking at you, Alex, are you listening at me?

Fisherman's Bend

I have forgotten. A small child was lost, intimidated it seems, he was chased by small children, he hid in a boat crying. Yes, that seems to have the truth. A small child, he remains nameless, would not come out so afraid he was. Afraid? Most afraid. And his father came forward to save him. His father? A certain father came forward, heard his cries and came forward. Rushed toward the boat and found him in under the bow. A true story! How does one little child become so scarified that he will not come out even to his own father? What strange reflection the father saw in the glasses of his son—his own self weaving in duplicate against the blue sky, cloned in the image of the beholder: schizophrenic and god. A sound against the rising of wind: the child's teeth rattling and shaking, the child clinging, immovable, deep inside, and this father's pleas unlistened to. His father attempted to save him, crawled forward himself under the tight bow. What would any other father have done? I should have gotten the saw and cut him out from the top. Trapped in the hull of a boat: first one, then there were two. A father has caught his shoulders foreside of the struts; a big man has kicked so hard from the inside trying to get the two of them out that he has brought down a beam. The hard point of it has fractured his leg. Tibia: compound. We will not think of that sound slugging away in the leg, at the inside. Your eyes have a strange look to them, Alex, that I wish you would give away. How many hours have we been here? I feel it, the blood now, rushing out my leg. I cannot move enough to tie off the vein. Don't think that. It is not your fault.

Horse Latitudes

We take us a feathered puffin wind out onto the lake—Bobby, Carlisle Casson and I—and Bobby insists we sing out "Sweet Marie" in applause of myself who has remembered to bring three sweaters and one tin can in case we might find a need—urgent or not—to bail this boat out. We get ourselves forsaken of the wind just once, ten minutes, no longer, long enough for Carlisle to invent and deride the end of every known escape; C.C. is brandishing one ice tea glass which he has forgotten to adhere to the dock. Horse latitudes! C.C., in a circumstantial dismay, shouts out. Then he is laying it onto us—on our first cruise—the most pathetic tale of animal destruction and becalmedness. Carlisle relates in pictorial terms: one fierce silence of wind fallen onto the ship and crew, riggings and boom. In his story, we are squatting windless at 33 degrees south of the equatorial divide, the crew put immediately to work at the oddities and enmities of safekeeping and repair of one boat. The capitan, Carlisle says, is a "good efficient bloke." Given no wind and fewer and fewer further instructions, we turn to singing and idling of hours, the making of tales, the telling of horrors, the checking of the sheet and the mast once again, the obser-

vation of the birds and sea creatures, the quibbling and jostling among friends, the skulking about in idleness, and the lightening of the load: our horses driven in a frenzy overboard, in a mist of wild animal screams. Our sail seems a mere bedsheet patched and rumpled onto blue sky; the lake lies out flat as a cardboard with the willow trees crouched down at its edges and frozen in the act of taking a drink. I am looking onto the taut walnut slopes of my husband's face as he picks up the lightest splinter of wood and tosses it overboard onto the rippleless sheen.

Now the house is a peanut at the edge of this dish; now I am laughing so hard, shaking my head, I have to put my glasses in my lap. The tears squeak down my face: "Hey, you two, you are only one-quarter mile from land any which way you look." I am laughing so hard I am lucky I don't fall out of the boat. "You're not going to jettison any horse, brothers! Unless you count me *as one when I dive home to eat my own lunch."*

When the wind cut us lose, we laughed ourselves sick. In these moments I was glad that the knee jerk had come onto him last winter to get his head, around nighttime, out of the searing neurosurgical constructs of his day-to-day and construct us a boat. He had followed the book that close: we did not even spring a leak. Leslie Bailey requisitioned the sails, and we waited a full winter while he built it up from clean lumber into pieces so as not to get us a hull big as a henhouse in the cellar and no way to grease the incubus out. Come spring, we spliced it together out back of the house. C.C. and Leslie helped haul it down to the dock.

They Shall Remain Nameless

In the story the character was gone though he moved through the scene. He had had a pretty fierce time of it, Alex. Looking onto it now we say, if only he had spoken up, got help from his friends which may be true enough and certainly is. But there is more to it than that. There is a blame to be laid. His eyes they were fixed and dilated as two tin pans in his head. He had himself a body, Alexei, yet he was dead. Every one recognized the truth in it, from many countries of disparate philosophies, all knew it the same: the spirit was gone from him by way of his pain. I have thought onto this for many months. No, for years and years. Thou shalt not kill.

So it has been said. There are no exceptions written into the verse.

Once a brother discovered blood plasma, how to obtain it and administer it. So I said in my speech. When he died, it was for want of a transfusion. Most cruel and ironic. He had been refused the transfusion in the hospital. Perhaps he did not have enough money? Perhaps not the right color? *I'm a blue man. Baby, why you burn down your brother's house?* Euphemisms growing like *E. coli* all over the place. Greediness of vision will break your heart in half. Bigotry come to have a narrow meaning. Why do I give you such a blatant example, Alexander? What is the reason it is more sad to hear of the inventor of plasma dying for want of a plasma due to color of his skin than to hear of another dying for want of plasma due to want of money or due to color of skin? Is not each life a life? Who are we to judge? We have here the bigotry of the races, of the riches, of the religions and of all their forms and sects, bigotry of the sexes, bigotry of the governments. We have the bigotry of the living and the dead. Don't now, Alex. Please don't.

Not six hours ago I stood at the back of the house. What was it I found when I got to your sounds? Is it this my own son curled up at my gut and how did we get here? We have been here so long I cannot once remember what it was we knew to be real. Once the dogs bayed up like this for my grandfather, once for my grandmother carried back without her husband to be entered by strangers and beat. And no one else knows your own torment, the way you see history. If you lay out a row of jumping beans in the sun, only a few will prove willing to move. Some say that is only because they have the wingless fly inside of them that won't let them be. They must speak for the rest. From life's first outrage, zeroing in on the end.

If I were to stick my foot through this hull, we would sink. Push / Don't

Do/nt push.

Spring summer winter and fall go rushing out. Of my leg. And it was a breach. No less certainly. Isn't it funny what the hell foolish predicaments we get ourselves in? By morning we will be laughing ourselves sick, if we don't find ourselves stone dead. Exposure being the ice pick of the four seasons known to get the life out. We will not think of that. Sweetly we rock on the waves though a storm is blowing up, our voices mere salt in the wind. Nearly sawed off these surgical fingers—indices both—in a slip with the band saw making the boat. Don't panic. Edwardo is also with us, charting our course. Don't now. Please don't. It isn't my fault. If I can kick our way out now, my how we'll swim, the sights we will see: fish deep along the bottom among the mottled pebbles, whiskers of the catfish and reeds, the bow of a boat, a mast pointing the way. To and fro we are rocking while up and down the valley the dogs bay up bay down in their tizzies following blind leads.

A Preponderance of the Small

In the middle of the ferry like some misplaced cornered animal, up against one of the small, white, starboard windows: Mary Moran. And in the pane: a ship, flat-black, rising up as if to overcome the window frame. The hull of the Japanese freighter, even in the downpour, had no sheen; and there on the deck, one man, middle-aged, in black slicker and hood, pitched about as if he were not attached, even in his innermost life, to anything. A sprinkling of gray-black whiskers sprouted from his jowled cheeks; and then the vision slipped away into a chalkboard sea.

It had been raining for three weeks—slick like milk and running off of everything. Still, it was nothing to compare with the weather of N——. A city: N——. A city of rain. Out of which she had begun to travel nearly every day by car and then by ferry to a summer job, all she could find that year. It was far away on an island that had been named most whimsically for reliable light, a state of grace.

On the bench opposite stood a newspaper sheet and from under it a pair of long slender jeans worn gray-white. The legs crossed, and there: two shiny, red, rubber boots ran to the knees. With the motion of the boat, the uppermost boot swayed with the waves; and Mary Moran could not keep from thinking again.

A September afternoon, it is their first autumn in N——, and Riley Moran comes home with a white cardboard pastry box. His thumbs loop around her belt, fingers drumming her waist. His breath is at the top of her head, slow and moving, a living thing. Rain slips down the window panes. Beyond the mullions painted white to tempt in light, the gutters clog again with detritus from the evergreens. Water overflows the pipes outside, washes past the window in a cascade. Mary takes hold of the tissue paper in the box. One of their favorites? *Pain au chocolat?* How ludicrous the sight in the bakery box: luminous gridded soles of the bright red, rubber infant's boots. A city of rain. Mary and Riley laughed out loud for the first time in over a week. Already they were under it—an autumn rain that they'd been told might not let up. Until June at least.

The crossing was rough that day, and Mary swayed both as she left and as she returned to her seat. In the bathroom several times she had had to brace herself so as not to fall down. When she sat by the window again, the newspaper dropped. "You know—" the blonde stranger said, casually, as if they'd just interrupted themselves. "All those mirrors in there are set so that, no matter how you look at yourself, you cannot see the back of your head." The woman's yellow-brown eyes looked right through her; and Mary, briefly startled, looked away.

Life in N——, so far from friends and family and their customs in the East— Well, in the beginning she had felt quite confident, for a short time. Soon all the dinner parties began to seem the same. The candles in the center of each cloth would make a spot of warmth against the sound of leaden droplets at the windowpanes, and then the quiet chant of conversation would begin. The women murmured only to one another, their dinner napkins clutched to their legs. A man gestured and then Riley, too, began to speak openly, though in a much subdued voice, and then another man, and another. For a time, she herself had offered opinions and anecdotes as she might have done at home, laughing or speaking in response to what had been said. No, it was not a matter of a lack of gracefulness or intelligence that caused the silence to fall. Heads turned to stare; they would not turn away. Finally she would glance again, silenced, toward the small flame drifting on top of the red wax stick. Surrounded by the others, she thought of mannequins without their collars or their wigs. After a time a snatch of conversation would catch her up again, and she would try not to hear. What an effort it was not to say a thing. She lowered her thoughts instead into the center of the candle's glow, at the space between wick and flame.

F I V E or ten minutes when the sun would come out! Once or twice a week toward very late spring! So clearly, even weeks later, she felt the horror of that day: of being caught up in business on the telephone at just the wrong time—it was about Dr. Chandler's second house, a business deal she had worked very hard to close. She came to the end of the cord as the white rectangle—light and airy—floated down across the room, falling in a panel onto the floor through the suddenly visible and glimmering dust. She would have rushed to stand dead center in its warmth. She reached out, but the light disappeared without her ever having entered it. She had no idea when it might again occur.

"It's no surprise then that everyone seems ethereal," she burst out finally to the mother of one of her daughter's little friends. "Why, your entire cranium is in a cloud," she laughed. "Mine, too. Look at everyone: the cliché's come true!" No one could deny it. The clouds were down around all of them, and they had nothing but a pervasive dark mist for air. The woman stared at her very harshly. And then—how Mary didn't know—the subject turned, as it often did, to the intricate studies that had been made in N—— of the proper ways to prune. It was only natural that such an interest should prevail; there was no dormant season in N——. Everything, in the rain, always grew.

Increasingly those first years, out through mist Riley stared, his eyes slightly glazed and his fingers trembling minutely until his cup began to chatter in his saucer and he set it down. He would sit straight up then and grip his knees. Not once would he stop looking into the milky sky as he stroked his legs. And then he began to joke about his joints, sad little jokes only to her. One weekend afternoon she had found him face down on their bed screaming silently. Lying on his stomach while reading, both his knees had locked straight. He had not been able to inch off the bed; when finally he did and was able again to walk, he had wrenching pain that did not subside.

Another month passed before Riley came home one evening, trying to make light of yet another session among the long coats and cool hands of the physicians of N———. The doctor that day had been in his early thirties, Riley guessed, with hair cut short and bristly. It was like a soft bath brush, Riley said. Riley described his appointment graphically for her, as if it hurt him to miss any part of the experience that might make a point.

"You can have it for twenty years—" the doctor told him privately. The two men, Riley said, leaned together toward the mysterious red tip of the doctor's pen. Like a small, bright, animal tongue, it tapped on Riley's folder while the doctor spoke. "You can even be in a wheelchair with it, and they'll tell you you're a fool for complaining. All their experience tells them what it is, but if it hasn't come up on the scanner yet they won't say a thing. They actually *lie* to their patients, I tell you! It's inhumanity!" And then the doctor caught himself. "Excuse me," he said looking at the pen quietly again. "Have you ever sprained your ankle?"

"Sure," Riley said.

"You know how that feels?"

"Yes, sure."

"A bad sprain?"

"Of course," Riley said irritably, looking into the doctor's fierce eyes.

"Ever hear a piece of chalk squeak hard up against slate?"

"Yes— But I don't see—"

"Can drive you nuts, eh? It hurts. Put that chalk squeal at the core of that sprain, right in the joint—"

"Why, yes!" Riley cried out.

"That what you feel?"

"Why, yes, that's it!"

"You got it in a few places now, right?" The doctor looked out at Riley from under the bill of his short-cropped hair. "Put that wracking pain in every one of your joints. Put it in every juncture of cartilage and bone you got—from your breastbone down to your feet. All up and down your spine, between every vertebra and the next, from your skull down to your tail. In your palms and your feet along the tendon sheaths—" The doctor shook his head; and it was then that Riley realized, uncannily, that they were of a similar age.

"What would *you* do?" Riley asked in a frightened voice.

It was at that moment that the resident flew into a truly unprofessional rage. Reciting it for her, Riley had tried to laugh at the doctor, but the attempt to joke fell flat; and he ended up repeating the doctor's words in a terror-stricken voice:

"What would *I* do! If I showed no radiological symptoms, man?" Riley's eyes were nearly frozen in his head, repeating it for her. "I?! I—for one—would count my blessings. I'd get out as fast as I could! You got no respect for your body, man? What the hell do you think a warning signal is?" The doctor tapped wildly on the streaming window pane. "Rain," he shouted. He tapped again with his pen. "Rain! Rain eats joints!"

"But they say I don't have it!" Riley cried out.

"That's right," the doctor jeered. "And a whole team of little fairies came along and locked up both your knees." The doctor said nothing further as he stood up to open the door. Riley swore to her that he had seen a little catch repeating itself then in the doctor's own slow gait.

It was that very next Sunday afternoon, after Riley had been to see the outspoken doctor, that Juliette had had a little friend over to play. Riley was in the bathroom giving a late night shave to his jaw when Mary told him about it as they were getting ready for bed. The bathroom door was partly closed, and Mary was busy herself as she called out the story to him:

She'd been scooping the layers of soggy pine needles from the front stoop when suddenly a moment of sun came over the yard. It was while she paused to bask in the light that Juliette and her little friend rushed past her toward the house, shading their eyes. "What's the matter?" she yelled after them.

"Acckkk!" they cried in a duet of the purest, most natural childhood disdain. Perhaps some insect or one of the immense myriad green slugs had presented itself to them, Mary thought.

"What is it, Juliette?" she yelled again into the house. "Come out and play."

"But the sun is out!" Juliette whined. "How can we *see* anything?" Mary Moran opened her mouth to speak. But suddenly she did not know what to say. The children were already inside singing a nursery song back and forth in rounds. She let them stay. Perhaps she herself was abnormal to think it odd. They had been in N—— for a good part of Juliette's small life. Even the child's spoken words had taken form while they lived there. Thinking back on it now on the ferry, she could for the first time take note of the tiny bandage she had seen on Riley's cheek while he lay over her that night. She knew finally that it must have seemed odd to him, too, a fact that he had allowed her to overlook. With him, staying in N—— was a matter of pride. Yes, everything had seemed quite ordinary everywhere else they had lived.

Again the woman called Carrie Turner nodded toward the rest room. Her hair was a bit longer then. How many years ago? Carrie's hair: sunny on the ends. And Riley was even then, on that first day of her job, already several months dead of an auto wreck. Mary was very alone with Juliette, their daughter, only three and a half.

The ferry captain was setting off the horn. The sound—a low bassoon—traveled just for a moment under her feet up through her bones. It was true about the women's room. Yes, she agreed, going over the details of the area. On the long makeup table the double-sided mirror ran up the center before a row of soda fountain stools that lined both sides. Two complete walls loomed as looking glass, multiplying everything. Though Mary Moran wasn't tall—five two, in certain shoes, maybe five three—even she had to lean toward the table mirror so as not to cut off the top of her obsidian bangs. It was clear you were meant to put on makeup at the table sitting down, to turn around standing up to comb your hair. Yes, she had agreed with the stranger, at the table you had to lean forward, until you almost touched your face to the picture of yourself, just to get the whole effect. And you could not for all the views, just as Carrie said, watch the back of your head.

Yes, Carrie said, Carrie's own grandmother, unprepared for bad seas, had situated herself—over twenty years before—on this same ferry at that cosmetics table behind the yellow varnish of the burnished ash door. She remembered the old woman always in a dignity of sculpted silver-blue hair with a pair of delicate glasses hanging on a fine silver chain like a thread from her throat.

And what sort was Carrie then?

Carrie: a child infused with the fevers of precociousness crept toward her grandmother that day in the lounge. The old woman faced away from the door, and Carrie saw the elbows as two points on a long swaying table. She saw the back and sides of a softly curled, blue, throbbing head cradled in the long, age-spotted, and beautifully thin hands. The reflection of her face was completely obscured by her back. Carrie remembered thinking it was as if her grandmother were sitting in front of a window instead.

The small Carrie growled like an animal that day with arms darting up in monstrous form. A Dracula! King Kong! And the old woman lurched in fright, gray-faced with a thorough sickness of the sea, swinging around on one of those low round stools, and nearly fell at what she saw. What ghoulish contortion was this in front of her? Small nostrils pulled up like two pits of hell, the lower red lids of the eyes wrenched downward in pouches of fluid or blood. A mouth unspeakably twisted.

By unknown grief. Or fear. The grandmother's horror was no less horrible.

Mortified at the sight of her grandmother's face, Carrie squealed wildly in return. She ran forward first in confusion, fell back and hit her head on one of the stalls. What a sight the frail old woman had made of herself on the boat, directed by the lurching mirror: the smudged purple cupid lips and each bravely attempted wobbling circumflex above the black feathered eyes, like nothing Carrie had ever known.

Carrie picked herself up, crying out in recognition and relief: "You look like a clown, Grandma!" At first the old woman didn't hear, and the child had the innocence to explain about the television freak with the canister of seltzer spray. When finally the grandmother understood, she streaked her face with flesh-colored tears. The young Carrie also sobbed, kneeling before one of those pedestals with her childhood face pressed into the warm trampoline of her grandmother's tight tweed skirt. The woman called Carrie sadly remembered that, she said, each time she went into a tavern and saw the row of floating silver circles and all the sad young men perched there, hanging like panting daffodils over the bar.

Mary's mother had worn them, the cupid lips, in New Jersey, Mary had said that day in casual reply. How anticlimactic her own story seemed as she went on: she could remember the scent as much as the feeling of her mother's creamy perfumed mouth brushing her small one when her parents went into the City to see a show. And once she had been the envy of her three sisters when she wore the same lipstick herself. It had been a necessity—to go with an early pair of heels that had pinched—viciously!—her toes. Cupid lips. They imagined whole rows of them swaying in the mirror in the bathroom, tilting with the rhythm of the ferry riding over waves in earlier years. So Mary Moran's first conversation with Carrie had begun.

E A C H day, an hour out of N——, the sky would begin to crack open over the car, and a sheen would appear on the little attachments that fasten the windshield wipers on. Then if Juliette were with her on rare occasion, again and again they lifted up their sunglasses, in unison, shouting, anxious to let the light in, too unaccustomed now to immediately submerge themselves. Most often she was alone.

Each day the car nudged into one of the parking lanes that sloped directly toward the water. There she would abandon it until the ferry came trudging as if on a thousand heavy boots to take her away. So near the ferry landing, so close for the daily quick call, Carrie's garden lay just the other side of the high hedge. If it had not been for that surely Mary would never have gotten to know her further at all. On Carrie's lawn each day floated the yellow disk of sun hat beside the low stone house. Here and there beneath the swaying trees, the blue grass was cut out as if by a compass, and from each circle beneath the elder trees grew an infant fruit with a strip of white cotton tied like a sling over its arm.

Near the house Carrie had planted a garden: bright mottled bursts of color among sunny, rough leaves. Large, grainy berries. A few tomato plants, too, Broccoli, and the dusty heads of cabbages. At the edge of the plot, the feathery tops of the carrots drifted along a tight line like a whim. And there the land dropped off under the brilliance of sun. Down the rocky cliff. Into a living, sparkling, sapphire sea. And beyond—toward the horizon? A purple island, then two, and the green and white ferry like a miniature house. Expanding moment by moment until it could carry Mary Moran away.

Carrie was accustomed to speaking quickly; and in the short time Mary had with her each day, whole years collapsed into one or two significant scenes. For a time Carrie had taken up scuba diving and had procured nearly all of her own food. She had been a mountaineer once and had climbed many of the highest peaks. One year she studied quite seriously the art of carpentry. Each of these avocations she mentioned so briefly that Mary was left with an image of Carrie frozen as if to the pages of a magazine.

That Carrie could build things herself was not a great surprise. Mary had had a friend in the East who had lost her leg while still an adolescent in a freak sledding accident. Many times she had seen that friend hoisting a wooden leg over the pine beams of a cabin she was building for her husband, her children, and herself.

Carrie crouched forward as she reached for a little crabgrass grown up among the marigolds. "Mary—" So few people in N—— called her by name, even now after these few years, what a pleasant shock it was! Like ice cubes rubbed on the pulse of your throat on a very hot day. Carrie's hat tilted back, and her tan face looked straight out. Carrie, too, had lived for a time in the darkness of N——, she confessed. "Why once, Mary, I was going out the front door when I saw something big and dark. It was moving!"

Mary sat down horrified on the edge of the cement and imagined her own front door. "What was it?" she asked.

Carrie laughed then: "Mary, it was my own shadow! Can you believe it? I hadn't seen it in months."

In astonishment Mary Moran looked at her new friend. Suddenly she realized that it was true; she had lived there and she had never noticed that there was not enough light in N—— for shadows to form. "Scared of their own shadows—" Mary said, running her finger along in a little trough of dry, hot dirt that day as a ladybug walked across her hand. "Why that's exactly what it's like!" Then she felt a little embarrassment; but for what or why, she couldn't say.

Carrie was fairly tall and lean with a wide-set stride and eyes that could turn, under her light brows, from golden brown to mahogany in the proper lights. She did not have a little girl face like you see in magazines. She had a strong facial structure—wide-boned through the cheeks and strong in the jaw—with perfect skin that went, in summer, from beige to golden brown like a piece of crackling in the bottom of a pan. She had straight white teeth. Perhaps she had friends. Carrie never mentioned a soul; and Mary thought it improper to ask.

Carrie stood up and patted the dirt off the back of her jeans. "I lived in N—— for seven years." She looked up at the clear blue sky and threw her head back with such joy that Mary did not know whether they laughed together or separately. The sky, was, after all, only the sky.

II

We drove across the peninsula toward the rain forest only to see the peaks of R—— rising up black out of a blue mountain fog. Everywhere the underbrush was tipped with orange and wine, and the trees themselves seemed thick in their dark evergreen coats. The ground spread in a damp brown cushion away from the road. The few deciduous trees had turned almost magenta now.

There was a false sense of glee in the two of us and even Juliette took it up, bouncing wildly in the back seat, pointing now at animals and trees, now screeching out their names, now singing along with the radio. It was the week she had taken it upon herself to cut her already short black bangs as a surprise. She had used my pinking shears, and she was a jagged sight. "Heron! Heron!" she screamed, and her funny little bangs flew up and down like teeth at the top of her face. And it was true: she had seen a heron: two elongated twigs for legs. A blue body like a feathered football. Long blue arms with extended wings and a curved thin neck. Its head turned to one side to display its scissored beak. Someone's lawn ornament.

"Not yet, Juliette," I said. "Not a real one this time."

"Heron!" she screamed, her head thrust forward between the seats. Together in front, Carrie and I sighed and smiled and nodded at her, and I reached back to pat her round flushed cheek.

We had a splendid time that week. We found a cheap room with a kitchenette, heavy pine paneling, hot water, and a picture window that was filled with the sea pounding onto a sandy yet boulder-strewn beach. Three sea stacks rose up out of the mist. As soon as we had unloaded the car, we pulled on our boots and heavy sweaters and prepared to set out. But I, who always planned now for rain, had—in my concern about finding another job and packing Juliette's things—forgotten my own gear. "What shall I do?" I cried with uncharacteristic helplessness.

With a paring knife Carrie cut holes in two plastic bags: one bag for my torso, the smaller one for the hood. When finally we drove off to where we would enter the rain forest on foot, Carrie peered at me from under the yellow brimmed plastic hat she had tied under her chin. "Why, you're the Plastic Pope," she laughed.

"Yes," I, too, laughed, passing it on, pointing at the peaked green-black plastic hood poking up between our front seats. "And there is the littler one." For Juliette's own yellow slicker had no longer seemed elegant to her after she'd seen what I wore, what Carrie had made.

"Pope, Pope, Pope!" Juliette cried out. And we looked very much the same.

It was then that Carrie made up a ditty Juliette has not forgotten to this day. The two of them seemed to be repeating it from that moment on, as long as Carrie was in our lives. First one of them would start and then the other would—in nonsense hocketing, their faces pressed fondly together, nose to nose. Carrie took hold of the edge of Juliette's makeshift hood and peered in at her face. On each word she tapped Juliette emphatically on the cleft in Juliette's chin.

"The exterior—" she sang.

"Of the interior—" She tapped again, and Juliette's little jaw was clenched with joy at every word.

"Of the fox terrier—" The rest came out not unlike a ribbon of paper rolling out of a machine:

"Is inferior to the interior of the exterior of the fox terrier!"

Even I, who hate repetition, was caught up in it. To this day I have tried to imagine what it could mean. We were interrupted in the chant that first half hour only once very seriously and that was when suddenly we all gasped and turned. Beside us, a crystalline field we had thought to be lovely early snow lifted up in a triangular piece into the gray sky. Snow geese flooded the window panes. The car shuddered with the flapping of wings. Heading south, the white wedge rose between heavy clouds as if borne on a sudden shaft of sun.

Carrie in the rain forest, in her yellow slicker and red, red boots, looked rather like an important piece of Juliette's most recent paste-in book. There she had fixed yellow bananas onto quiet black and white New England scenes. A cushioned path of foliage disintegrated infinitely beneath our feet. "We're wading a swamp—" Juliette sang ahead of us. And over us still, far up, were the ascending trunks of trees and then there were branches, and then the tops touching perhaps the light up there in distant pinnacles over which the rain came, sifting and sifting until it fell on us who ran like smaller animals among the lower limbs and the great hanging mosses, the man-sized ferns.

The undergrowth, though present, did not seem to cut us off. It came in clumps like pleasant times among the mossy trunks. The air was dim with the thick draperies of further moss. We wandered quietly for some time, talking of books we'd read that week. It was a joy to speak again with someone who shared that interest and was not reticent. How is it that in one moment life goes one way and in the next turns another and most terrible way? We were just discussing *The Idiot*, when we noticed in horror that Juliette had disappeared.

We heard no echoes; we did not hear her small repetitive voice. Each time I opened my mouth to call in that shadowless wood, the syllables disappeared, absorbed by the hideousness of mosses, the constantly decaying wood, and the terrible parasitic forms. Juliette's large eyes, so like Riley's, her short zigzagged bangs, all of her, had been torn from the scene. For what must have been a quarter of a mile we walked stiffly, our arms cast down at our sides, until there came a moment when together Carrie and I turned toward one another and startled ourselves, each with the other's face stricken featureless with grief. My future then, wretched and alone, without Riley or Juliette, seemed in my despair somehow complete. I would live in N—— permanently, a mere shell without need for light or response, the cradle of my own unhappiness.

But no less suddenly, out of the lower blurred regions of a giant fern: the elfin face! the jagged line of her bangs! Immense dark full lashes, a dimple blinking on and off in one startling cheek. Onto the path in her little plastic rain suit she sprang in the childish surprise she had planned for us. "When Daddy died—" Juliette squealed. Chilled, we halted in our joy. Her baby arm shot above her, pointing high, high— Where did the projection stop? Carrie and I stared after it, following the pointing mitten into the silence of the firs. "When Daddy died," my small daughter sighed, "he went—Up— Up— Up—" I caught my breath, and Carrie touched my hand. High, so high, in the folds of the trees, where my daughter pointed, there would be a little wind, and sun. Perhaps I was suddenly in that moment much too stern with her. The bright image of her face dissolved in tears. I knelt in the damp mosses and tried to explain how we must cling to what we have and let the others be taken away. I made no sense perhaps, I know— or all the sense in the world, I could not be sure.

I put out my hand for quiet then, and Juliette held to me. The great blue herons were already lifting their stilts out of the lavender mist; and then after several minutes, in stark black and white markings, two harlequin ducks tilted first one way and then the next as they angled past, gaining height so slowly they seemed not to depart. The sky did not open for them; the rain did not cease. Juliet brushed her cheek back and forth against my sleeve as we looked after them: two dots against a sky of milk.

Only one other event do I remember from that day. Julie has always exhibited a fondness for animals—lost or otherwise—a trait which I, as a child, also shared. Along the roots of the colonnade trees she had found a banana slug. It was yellow as a ripened fruit and just as long as one. Behind it, a trail of spittle; on its head, two little horns. If it had had a shell—it would have been a snail, Carrie slowly explained.

As she spoke she tapped her foot as if each word were attached to a music only she could hear. The shell, she said, had been incorporated into the animal itself and had become merely a lung; it had no home at all—except inside where it breathed. I don't know why I mention it, except perhaps to explain how interesting, and interested, Carrie could be for both Juliette and myself. Carrie did not speak of loneliness that day in the woods.

That night in our cabin Juliette went to sleep with her head on my leg—as she often did on nights of storms or bad dreams. She had her own blanket over her and on the top of that was Frank, the doll, who lay in turn on Juliette's hip. I suppose to Carrie we looked so happy all together, and yet in our evening zigzag all I could think of was our missing part. Carrie propped herself up on the other bed on all her pillows. Out on the ocean a storm was whipping up. We had turned out our lights, but the motel's searchlight shone onto the beach. Even from our beds we saw the lines of furious white froth, here, then there, cutting across the dark.

"I've decided to take it by the ears!" she laughed suddenly. There flashed her immense smile in the dim light that fell in from the illumination of the beach.

"What's that?"

"I've decided to have a child, too."

"I didn't know there was anyone right now—" I said.

"There isn't. I worked it out with a friend." She plucked with her hand at the sheet and went on in quite another voice: "Finally I said to myself: 'Carolyn, you feel like a rind, so there! So what is a rind for, you fool? Where is the fruit?' All my problems were solved at once." She stared over the sleeping Juliette with her ragged Frank into my face. "It only takes the imagination, Mary! And the will to live!" She looked a little terrified then. "That's it, isn't it? Don't you think?"

"I think it's very exciting!" I whispered, more concerned than anything. "We'll have a shower," I laughed awkwardly. "But you'll have to come to N—— where the real showers live—"

She plucked at the sheet. "Oh, gee. I wish you were keeping your job. I wish you could."

"I know," I said. "We'll have to make an effort." I reached for her hand, but the distance between the beds was too great. "Not just promises, but the real thing."

I don't know why but I told her quite suddenly about Riley then—how he had driven off the bridge one night coming home from work, how they had said the car seemed not to brake but rather to speed up even as it veered toward the rail, broke through, made its arch in the air and split the water in half. "Riley was silver. Like a fish," I said, and I began to sniffle very quietly. I couldn't help myself.

Carrie leaned across her covers. "What was that last, Mary?" Carrie whispered. "I'm very sorry. I understand how terrible it must have been, but your voice dropped just then—at the end—I didn't hear—"

Juliette's head moved slightly on my leg, and it was automatic how I pulled her covers up. "The car was silver," I lied. I couldn't say it again. There were tissues in the bedside table. "The car was silver like a fish."

"Was it suicide?" It was the first time anyone had talked with me about it face to face. My sisters had tried over the telephone. They were broke, like me, or they would have come out. I know they would have come. They had tried to get together enough to send just one of them, or to bring us home; they were going to take out a loan. But I told them not to. Where would the need end? If it had not been for Juliette they might have been able to pay my fare. We live so far from anyone; it's as if we are on the edge of the world, on a dark dissolving precipice.

"Do you think it was suicide, Mary?" Carrie murmured again.

I stroked the top of my daughter's head. Beneath her lids her eyeballs were tracking back and forth over sights I would never see. From out here, each eye looked as if a tongue were moving inside someone's cheek. I stroked her bangs. She did not wake up; she was still used to both her parents' affection even in her sleep. I looked over at Carrie who seemed so secure— even in her loneliness. I dabbed at my face. "For almost a year I thought it was. Until last week."

Carrie's blue flannel arm stretched toward me. I knew what it meant. Out the window it was difficult to distinguish in the motel's marked light the mercurious sky from the beach.

"But you don't think so now, Mariette?" She had taken to adding and dropping syllables over the summer when she felt concerned or affectionate. She said it again—"Mariette?"

I looked back into the room toward her. "I didn't know until a week ago when I banged my knee on a cabinet. It hurt like mad. *Poor Riley,* I said thinking of him again, and then I understood—for the first time—what happened to him."

I had told her about Riley's health, about the single episode with his knees; but it had been some time before. She fingered the lace on her sleeve. She said, "You shouldn't try to imagine how it was any more, Mary— You'll always be wrong most likely, and probably you'll imagine it much worse. They say natural adrenaline is a wonderful thing. Imagine him hallucinating when he went." And then she said a very peculiar, almost infuriating thing; she was not afraid to be ridiculous. She was not selfish in that way. "Think of him believing he was coming into you," she said.

I started to cry softly then and Juliette, as if instinctively, wrapped her fingers around my thumb. It is only now that I begin to wonder whether she understood that I had come to know that Riley had *not* committed suicide, that his knee had frozen that day on him the way it had that one afternoon on the bed. Now I no longer know. Perhaps the thought of it grew large in her mind: he was fleeing his pain. Time and again I have turned the whole conversation inside out.

"He didn't want to leave you, did he?" Carrie said.

I shook my head and blew my nose pathetically.

"Of course he didn't," she said. "Don't you ever, ever think that again." She stroked the blanket with her hand.

When Juliette and I left her off later that week at her house, it was already dark. We had become engrossed in watching deer in a glade and had started for home quite late. Perhaps it was that alone— But now I think it was more.

N E A R L Y three months after she met Carrie—in fact, she had come from coffee with her not forty minutes before— Mary Moran had an incident with herself in a split-level she was previewing near Sheepshead Bay. The house was to go up for sale at the beginning of the week. It was a rather large house—the size her husband Riley would have preferred, if not the style. The whole house nestled around a fireplace in a room downstairs and another upstairs in the living room. It was when she went into the kitchen and looked into the sink at the metal garbage grinder that she thought absurdly of Riley again.

That day Mary Moran sat down on the kitchen solarium and cried. It wasn't even a house they might have bought together. The ceiling fixture had holes in it so that light came out in a spray: stars caught inside a globe for good. *Riley, why did you do it? It isn't fair.* Familiar words she cried that day. Looking into the scattering of that light, all she could think of was his beautiful hair: how it had gone prematurely silver like tinsel all over his lean body and in the little mustache like a brush on his slightly thick warm face.

It was quite an unfortunate day. The split-level was the only house she saw that afternoon, and she had to go home with a sense not only of grief, but also defeat in her soon-to-be-completed job. When she drove off the ferry and up the ramp, heading back toward N——, she did not notice whether the house of her new friend was lit up or not.

But you should have stopped, Carrie said.

I wanted to get home to Juliette.·

That made every kind of sense, they agreed.

Why did she stay in N—— then?

The house she and Riley had bought with such great excitement, suddenly, she could not now afford to keep nor give up;

she could not gather enough money to move them anywhere, let alone back East.

Carrie was at her loom; and Mary Moran, bathed in light, watched the shuttle go back and forth. The machine made a comforting dull thud as regular as breathing in the room. It was late in September as Mary remarked that she had bad dreams. She had seen a bum in the Square in N—— the winter before. Still she could not get the sight out of her head. Every night now as she prepared to return for the office position she'd found in N—— she dreamed it just as it had happened in real life: with Juliette she had taken their stale loaves of holiday bread downtown. How generous Mary's sisters had been with baked goods during the holidays. How sorry they were, they wrote in their cards, that Mary would not have their company nor even a white blanket of snow to take the dampness from the cold, to make them feel at home.

The leftover cakes the two of them could never finish by themselves, the cookies with nuts they both eschewed, and the gifts of fruitcake which only Riley had taken seriously: these they left in the garbage baskets scattered around the area. On the second floor of one of the newly sandblasted old buildings, the family took up their post.

Out through a large window on the landing they peered, just in time, to see one tattered young man stretch out on a central bench below. The pink and gray heel of his foot protruded like a coin from his shoe onto the old, brick, pigeon-cluttered rectangle that would again be so attractive to tourists in the muted hue of summertime. "Oh, look, Juliette!" Mary Moran cried that day, and every night now in her dreams. "He has one of Georgie's cakes!" A winter drizzle puffed at the large glass pane. Even from so far away, Juliette could count the little red dots of the cherries and the green and orange candied peel. They saw him take up the whole thing between his raw hands.

"He's going to eat it! He's going to eat it now!" Juliette squawked, leaping up and down.

Out from one of the new law offices just then a woman stuck her extravagantly curly head. "Whisk, whisk,—" she cried. But mother and daughter had their faces pressed against the plate glass pane. Below, the man motioned and an older one appeared as if from outside the picture frame. Their faces melted behind the young one's stained gray hat, as the two of them bent over their find, and then the perfect little rum cake was rent in half. "Look!" Juliette cried. "They know how to share. They say thank you and please!"

Mary Moran smiled on as the newcomer shoved his portion into one of his innermost layers of yellow shirts. Almost beatifically the first bum lay on his back—as if on a board, his arms straight out from his trunk. Then the second half of their cake was ripped to bits before their eyes. The old man laid out the crumbs all over the unfortunate friend. Pigeons soared from the rusty brick to land on him. How very gray he was! As if in signature, as seen from above, one great cross seethed on the square below with life.

III

For weeks I tried to call after I left my job, but the phone rang on and on. Several times on Saturdays Juliette and I got our dark glasses out of the drawer beside the sink and made the northern drive again, thinking we would catch her by surprise or scout her out. Juliette bounced beside me in anticipation of seeing again her special friend. I heard the chant of the fox terriers, including now their anteriors and their posteriors. But when we arrived, Carrie's curtains were drawn. No one answered our knocks and shouts. She had moved the key she once had kept for us. Juliette stood on her toes, her small face and hands pressed to the glass storm door as she peered in at the sealed inner planks. I stared down at the top of her glossy cap of hair. "Maybe Carrie has gone away to have her baby, Juliette," I said. "Think of that." But Juliette would not look up at me. She would not say anything. She rested her head in my lap all the way back into N——.

T H E woman—huge with pregnancy—hurried away at my cries, for several blocks, losing ground as she went, until finally I took her by the sleeve and swung her around to find nothing but the dead-white face of someone who lived constantly in N——. And then one day, nearly a year later, unexpectedly I did come across Carrie in N——. She wore an immense silver raincoat—shiny like mercury—and shaped like a tent. Out of the collar, under a vibrant red umbrella was Carrie's face; and before her, under her breasts was the shape of her child. We threw our arms around each other as well as we could, the umbrella upended, a red splash at our feet. We went down the walk, our arms crooked together, as cozy as old times. "What are you doing here?" I asked. "You hate N——! I've been trying to contact you since August before last!" I noticed then that she was a bit pale in the face, but it was winter; and we were, after all, in N—— where everything seemed indistinct. It had been raining for half the year now, gently, continuously; but no one I knew had talked about it. We jostled along—I with Carrie in her awkwardness. Without her enthusiasm she looked quite unlike her usual self.

"Don't you feel well?" I asked. "Shall we sit for a bit?"

"I'd like you to take me for a ride," she said. If it had been a bright day somewhere, there would have been a rosy glow from the umbrella cast over her face. "Like the other time," she said. "You and Juliette. I've been alone too much. I've missed you both."

We hunched along the gray streets. I suppose the walks and alleys, and avenues, were flowing with water then; it was winter so they must have been. I didn't much notice such things any more. I kept my head down and went my way. Carrie's umbrella was the only one on the street. I, too, had given up the unwieldiness of such things and had purchased a fine ankle-length raincoat, high boots, and a waterproof hat. I had not yet seen my way to wear the clear cones the others wore—the ones that came down over the face and neck. I had tried one on once. It was not unlike looking out from the ledge behind a small waterfall. Constantly the plastic streamed in front of the face. Looking in at the others, I thought: why, any one of them might be weeping and no one else would notice it.

"Really, I mean it—" she said again as we hurried to meet her bus. "I'd like so much to go for a ride with you and Juliette."

In elation I squeezed her arm in my elbow as we crossed the street for the station. I felt her great bulk against my sleeve. "Of course we will!" I cried. "You silly goose! We've been crazy with worry without seeing you." I threw my arms around her again, and I swear I felt her infant hammering like a fist between my stomach and hers. When I think back on that day I remember Carrie as being particularly quiet, but then I had been away from my kind for some time, I told myself. I, too, had grown silent. Perhaps it had been my fault.

C A R R I E swore she was not due for another month and a half when we set out on our trip; and she clearly needed to get out. Juliette was thrilled all that week. She had made a present for Carrie—a ring of construction paper flowers to "grow" around Carrie's yellow sun hat. It surprised me that Juliette thought of Carrie as living always in summertime. Seeing Carrie with the paper flowers strung around her neck, I realized that I had thought that myself.

I suggested that we drive farther into sunny territory since we were already halfway to the most reliably bright portion of the county when we picked Carrie up. I had already felt the intoxicating warmth on my face. But Carrie wanted to repeat our former excursion. She had her heart set on our driving again into the rain forest where there had been no question for either of us that it was rain that we had seen and its effulgence, its putrefaction, its lush parasites. It had been—the first time—like looking in on something hideous, something decadent and rich. But it was not for that, I think even now as I look back, that she wanted to go there again. Nostalgia, yes. And, I think, she wanted to see from that same room where she had told me about her hopes, the dim daytime light broken by waves. I think she wanted to lie in that same bed and feel the sharp sudden kicks just under her ribs. She wanted to go only for one night, a Saturday; and I was pleased not to have to deny her. Friday nights we are so exhausted and Sunday is always bad with having to get Juliette and myself ready for the week. Saturday was best.

On and on we drove, going farther and farther from sun into the territory of immense trees. Juliette plagued us with songs about birds, about insects, trees and other things: Ricky Ticky Terry / Ate a little berry / Ricky Turtle Terry / Wasn't very hairy / When he ate Ricky Ticky Terry / Who ate the hairless berry / But Ricky Ticky Turtle Terry / Grew very hairy / AFTERWARDS!

It was then that I realized how much time had passed. One autumn we had been in the rain forest. One winter had gone, and now here was another. I found myself counting the months backwards, despite myself, looking for an explanation of Carrie's pregnancy. Juliette in her precociousness was a great help.

Patiently and calmly Carrie explained in response to Juliette's ceaseless questioning that she had undertaken an advanced carpentry course after we had last seen her— busying herself, I assumed, during the time when she had been trying to establish a pregnancy or find a partner for herself. She had learned also, she said, in a survival course to walk lightly in the woods without making the twigs snap. Juliette asked her about her baby's father and was only partially satisfied to find that he was a very nice man from New York. Was he an architect? Juliette wanted to know; Riley had been studying to be one. No, Carrie said. He was a very nice businessman who lived in New York. And how had she met him? On the ferry, Carrie said. Oh, Juliette said. And was satisfied.

"Does he want to have an interest in the baby?" I asked.

"That isn't part of it," Carrie said.

"I see," I said, and I watched my hands tilting on the steering wheel, moving through the landscape.

N o w we were following under the hanging mosses, driving rapidly. The sun shot through a cleft in the mountains just as we were hurtling on the brim of the lake. How like fire it was— burning there in the olive water as Carrie and Juliette slept.

Even in her great bulk Carrie had managed to crawl into the back seat. I thought at that moment, and thought yet again, of a picture she'd shown me of herself in Switzerland at the edge of a road, with all her climbing equipment, a pick-axe in her hand, a Scandinavian sweater and hat with a little pompom on top of her head. It was all like a pose in an outdoor catalog. And then I let the thought of it go and relaxed in the sudden peacefulness. Juliette was snuggled up with her, my coat thrown over the top of them, their heads poking out. Juliette whistled a little in her sleep, and I remember thinking that I hoped she was not coming down with a cold or something Carrie might catch.

Juliette had wrapped her thin arm over my coat, over Carrie's stomach. Carrie's arm stretched out over the great hard ball that was part of herself, and held to my child. They were like two figures sewn to the opposite sides of a pincushion, the tall one and the little one, their hands clasped.

It was mid-afternoon when I saw Juliette's tousled head popping into the mirror again. Her black hair stuck out like spikes in several directions; and her face had lost its definition with her sleepiness. How strange that I do not remember more about our excursion. That is the last image that will come to me: Juliette's sleepy face dead center in the road we had just traveled through, hanging like a little icon over the billboards for cigarette sales and the asbestos-sided shacks of the Indians. Later that day we hiked along the beach and talked as we always did. We must have made some reference to Carrie's baby. The thought of it now makes me unhappy. How she must have pretended joy, how foolish it all now seems.

Mostly I recall her standing in her own kitchen, after our return, leaning against the wall, her slender hands on her stomach. I was preparing soup of the leftovers we had brought back from our overnight. We had built a fire in her fireplace; and even in the kitchen we could enjoy it, as it was the kind with a double hearth that is so lovely and adds so to the value of a house on the market. That was the thought I was having—how I might have sold such a house, how I would have presented it—when Carrie began to confide in me. Juliette was in the den watching the television. Perhaps Carrie had waited for this one moment of solitude. "I have been to the doctor," she said. I looked up from the little striped crescents of celery, the green-black lace of the parsley, the creamy thickening broth to see her. "Something terrible is happening," she said.

"Why, what is it, Carrie?" I asked in fright. But even then it seemed to me that perhaps she was just overly worried as I had been toward the end of my time with Juliette. A human being can only be expected to stretch so much. And then she said it. I will never forget that moment, the way the spoon seemed not to be able to cease on the bottom of the pan, the way I could not breathe at the sight of her tremendous, ripe body. For just a moment her head lay on its side directly on top of her own belly, and a tear ran out of the one eye across the bridge of her nose and into the other. "But, Carrie?"

"I am going blind," she said, and she shut her eyes and leaned her heavy bulk back against the rough plastered wall. "I have known it for almost six months. I wanted to call but—" Then she began to sob. "I knew I should have an abortion," she cried in my arms, "but I got paralyzed—with hopefulness and disbelief."

She had shut up all her curtains trying to learn to live without light. She had taken to wearing blindfolds and crawling about the floor hunting for pins she had scattered there. "What if the baby got pins in her mouth because I couldn't see them? Because I couldn't find them in time!" She could open jars now and tell what was in them by smell. She had installed safety catches in all the cabinet doors. Over and over she had groped her way into the basement, washing small loads of her own laundry—with the scarf tied tightly around her closed eyes. They could do nothing for her, she said. It could take a long time or it might happen in one eye, or both, overnight.

It was a very long weekend as we stayed on that extra day, but I could not convince her to come with us. That was the last time, but one, that I saw her. She promised to be at her house the following week; we would come visit. When we arrived, after our long drive, no one answered. All our efforts to find her failed.

T H E R E had been burnings—grains and berries, books, personal furniture, and surplus goods. No one seemed to acknowledge this in our city, though it was a continual topic on the national news. At work I tried not to let on how it sickened me. The front seat of my car was loaded down with books when once again, almost compulsively I pulled into her drive. I had been only twenty minutes away. I suppose I did not really expect Carrie to be there; yet when she did not answer the door I felt my spirits sink. On a whim of hopelessness I stopped to ask after her at the little grocery where she shopped.

The lines were still visible where a wall had been knocked down and the plaster not smoothed but painted over at the defunct junctures before the shelves and dry goods had been put up. I took up a newspaper and a small plastic dinosaur for Juliette and leaned over the counter toward the heavy man I had seen supervising, if not owning, the store a few times before. I could not tell whether his glasses were the old kind or part of the new rage for the old. He looked over the top of his lenses to survey the territory almost automatically when I asked for her. "The lady is building her house," he said.

"You've seen her!" I cried, feeling very much as I had when standing at Carrie's front door, listening to the first faint rings of the bell going off throughout the rest of the house. Perhaps people and things did not just disappear. The storekeeper's elbow sat on the top of his cash register; his head rested on his palm, the rugged flesh of his sunburned cheek brushing his wrist.

"This part of the woods doesn't suit her anymore." I couldn't make out whether he was glaring at me or extending sympathies. He took my change.

"But where is her house?"

"Up around Old River."

"In the woods?!"

"That's right—" He stared a long while at the wedding ring I still wore. I put my one hand under the other. He said, "That is the word we have."

"But, it rains night and day up there!" I burst out, in spite of myself. "She loves it here!"

"She and the child are moving up there to get away."

"She's had her baby already then?"

"Up to her house, I expect, yes. Up to her solo house she is."

I saw him staring aimlessly again where my own hand was wrapped around the rubber dinosaur I had for Juliette. "Good thing that isn't for real," the man said softly, tugging at his cap. "You've got a might good throttle on it."

"It's for my little girl," I said, shoving it into my purse. "You must know where along Old River she lives then?" I asked quietly.

"Miss Carrie a friend of yours?" he asked.

"Of course," I said but then a shiver ran up my back. "And we have business. I sell real estate. Doesn't she ever come home to pick up her mail?"

Absentmindedly, he prodded with his forefinger along the inside of his lower lip, moistening it. He thumbed through a stack of receipts then and for a moment I thought he was looking for her address. He did not move his other arm, nor his head from its resting place over the cash machine. His eyes swung left, then right. "Nope, they got a box brim full of first mail and junk fliers down at the post office. Box is big enough to hold a stuffed chair. And maybe a hassock. If you were to lay it on its side, I expect a hassock would fit there alongside the back of that chair—resting on the seat. No, Miss Carrie is not down to the post office panting for a look at her messages."

I tugged quietly at my ear. My elbow seemed to stick at my waist and I, too, rested my cheek on my fist. A faded construction paper wreath dangled from the pull loop on the window shade. Berries had been drawn in furious red crayola into the wreath, perhaps by this man's own child. "Who is the father of her baby? He might know where she is."

He shrugged then and his eyes squeezed up with delight. "Beats me." He had a short bark in the middle of his laugh and I could not make out what it meant. "Christ," he said. "If I guessed, I'd guess it to be the one and only."

"Pardon?" I asked and I shifted my head to my other fist.

"The very one and the very only—Sky King!" he cried out. "Why, who else?" And then he laughed again very harshly. "Sky King," he laughed— "the Good Lord."

My foot rocked against the linoleum where I could feel it curling toward the bottom edge of the counter. "Why's that?" I asked. "Surely in a little town like this you'd at least hear where to find her."

"That's exactly right," he said. "You think you see ears on this head in front of you, but I'm here to tell you that's just one of your illusions. I keep both ears flat to the ground. If she'd had a new address, I'd have heard it. If there'd been a father I'd have knowed it. That's what I'm telling you: that Captain Kirk must have done it. Or the Ghost. Who knows? Maybe a gang of gnats done it. But no one in this town worked up Miss-Miss Carrie. That is the final word, thank you—the story as we know it." He wore a green net shirt over his heavy middle, the thick brown hairs on his chest showing through and the pink nipples apparent as dimes in the grass. His green visor was turned around backwards as if he were trying to keep the sun from the back of his neck.

"Thank *you*," I said in return and turned to go.

"Maybe 'twas out of town help!" he called after me. "I do expect it was!"

It was many months before I found her. They say that she cannot have died more than four hours before I arrived. But that does not address much of anything. Certainly it does not take into account the package I found when I tried to collect myself in the bathroom after the police arrived.

"S T A R - N O S E D moles fly overhead the dead," I murmur, thinking endlessly of it now.

"What did you say, Mommy?"

"Star-nosed moles go to bed—"

"What?"

"—when their mothers tell them. It's a story, Julie, like 'Snow White' or 'The Man Who Ate Chicago'."

"Oh," she said.

"With a moral, if we could only find it."

"Oh," she said.

I was not feeling at all well the day I went to visit her—a kind of influenza was still clinging to me as I turned off exactly where her map, drawn by what assistant?, indicated. It was almost nine o'clock when I did so. To the sound of pelting rain I turned and drove straight into the bowel of the rain forest. It was so completely dark under the trees that I found myself reaching to turn on my bright lights before I had even gone a few yards. As the windshield wipers clicked the seconds, I could not stop hearing my own private voice saying a number each time they snapped in front of me. I found myself thinking then only of my work, the surprise I had had that week, and my intense depression over it.

On Wednesday I had begun counting memos—as I was required to do several times a week—promptly at 8:00 A.M. As always I attempted to finish by ten. There could be as many as a thousand memos. While I worked, I imagined the other junior executives engaged in the task, lined up alongside me in our glass-fronted boxes in a display of generosity for our underlings to see. It was the only explanation I could find for such waste and inefficiency. In the end, that image had become important to me: all of us up there together doing menial work that might otherwise have been passed down. It made me feel as if I were part of a system that could be scaled without loss of humanity. Indeed I would see every once in a while one or two of my women glancing up over their office machines at me, and I would smile a little, wryly, to set an example and to encourage them in case they should be contemplating a similar rise. But that week my entire understanding of the company changed.

I had been sitting in the leather arm chair that the company provided for me, beginning the weekly count, when my coffee was served as usual alongside the several butter cookies I had chosen that day. Perhaps I had eaten two of them, I can't be sure. My image of the other junior executives—all the clean young men—lined up along the wall beside me in their own cubicles, all of us in our individual picture frames, was especially comforting to me, I had been feeling so terribly alone. A running tabulation like a ticker tape clicked at the back of my mind. Every once in a while I would swing toward the workers in my division—my crew, as I thought of them—and then the other way to look out over the precipitous sights of N——. It was while I was turning that I caught the smallest unexpected fragment of cookie in my throat. Violently I then began to cough and choke.

Slowly it seemed, the heads of the hundred workers in my division rose to look at me, but I could not control the wrenching spasm. I seemed to bark in terror like an animal. Finally I was forced to break ranks and rush in embarrassment from my cubicle to the drinking fountain at the far side of our vast room. The eyes of the entire company turned on me then: hundreds of women in all the lower divisions watched my dilemma and my flight. I am conscious still of how close I came to choking to death, of how the entire group looked on as one, as if from a television screen, stagnant, indifferent in their chairs.

For the first time as I returned to my transparent cubicle, I had the chance to see morning activities from the workers' vantage point. Beside my antique table and its little coffee tray and cookies, beside my stuffed chair and hassock, in front of the desk, was the foot-high sheaf of memos I had been counting when I had my attack. In the lineup of junior showcases, up and down the row of cubicles there were similar sets of furniture. But in them sat no one counting out memos for the sake of company unity. Here, there, they were speaking to clients. Others engaged themselves actively on the telephone. Four offices were completely empty while their occupants congregated in the office two doors down from mine, drawing production charts on mechanized boards that reeled up into the wall. Not one other individual among the junior executives had a menial stack such as mine beside his desk. And yet I had had—well, I will not go on about my qualifications and the prizes I had won.

A s I drove up the dissolving road toward my newly blind friend and her baby, the rain fell even more heavily. The windshield wipers worked continuously and then there was only the merest remembrance of a soft green light beneath the hanging vines. Somewhere among these trees, there would be cougar, bobcats, and black bear. Juliette and I had seen the front print of a mountain lion in books: the four smaller pads pressed into the doughy mud of the photograph and then the larger one in back like a fist. Squirrels flew at night high up in the trees and red-back mice ran lightly among the upper branches. Quite suddenly, then in front of the car, just as I was making a turn, a blacktail deer seemed to crystallize at the side of the road.

Immediately I regretted not having brought Juliette along. At home her drawings of our studies hung on the refrigerator: squirrel with feathered wings flying between minute stars of rain, mice on branches among thick clouds, eating stalks and leaves. She had never seen or even perhaps imagined a deer so close that she might have reached out and touched its pure white antlers with her hands.

Snaking in at the end of a mud road three and a quarter miles long, I drove onto Carrie's property just as she had written I would. The house was set, just as she'd said, into a brief clearing among thick draperies of moss. They hung down almost like theatrical banners from a height of several stories or more from the lower boughs. The house had been very clearly depicted in her note, although perhaps someone had only described it to her. Perhaps she had had a chance to see the house she'd planned for herself. It was a small structure with a very steep roof. Already the preliminary stripes of the bracket fungi were beginning to climb its new wood. How carefully the house was situated on the rise of the hill, alongside a narrow, active river, just at a kind of plateau. A pinfeather of smoke twisted upward among dim trees.

For the sake of the new baby I had hesitated about coming at all. I had reached her finally by telephone but she would not hear of my postponing my trip and I could not hang back, ill or not, once I heard her voice. How Juliette would have squawked and leapt at the sight of the house Carrie had built, at the woods themselves and their gloomy fantastical qualities, the natural comic aspects of them: especially the otters floating on their backs in an eddy of the flooding river. There on its slick stomach the nearest one held a rock—the size of a soccer ball—between its front flippers—for ballast, I thought, or for use later in cracking open its afternoon lunch.

As I turned off the car and put on my rain hat, I chastised myself again for not having let Juliette come with me to see the animals jetting back and forth in the downpour beside Carrie's house. I had been self conscious about dealing with Carrie's new blindness, about worrying over Juliette's impressions, her innocent brutal candor. It seemed unfair of me; Carrie and Juliette were also friends. And, of course, I had primarily refused to bring her for selfish reasons, because of my cold, because of the noise she would blithely and naturally make that would only have spurred on my irritation and headache. I had been trying not to think about my discomfort on the way, but I had been dabbing at my face nearly the whole time. I had barely been able to breathe.

T H E elementary hook was the kind you might find on a screen door or a shed, high at the top to provide admittance for adults, to keep children out. It was secured in the outside hasp. It seemed natural to assume that Carrie had gone out somewhere—nearby, of course, hooking the door in this way, rather than using a key, so as to keep animals out. I had heard of scavengers—bears, porcupines and raccoons—slipping into people's homes and eating through a winter's supplies in an afternoon, but it had seemed a wonderful pioneer story for the entertainment of a child.

The house was very neat, and it was clear that she had had other people in mind, too, when she decorated it for visitors and friends. There were a few of her smaller weavings on one wall and a larger red and yellow, vivid one. In her own room the bed was spread with a red and white Amish quilt. A bright abstract print of a painting—I can no longer recall the artist's name, it was not one you would immediately know—hung on the highest living room wall.

I peeked into the back bedroom and saw the cradle she, or someone, had very carefully made and in it the little bundle under a yellow blanket turned on her stomach, resting quietly. Over the crib, a mobile of pastel plastic animals turned slightly on the breeze I had created with the door. I remember how thoroughly I smiled at seeing her there—Carrie's baby—how I held myself back from going in to hold her, waiting until Carrie returned so that she could present her to me herself. It was the kind of understanding that we seemed to automatically have had about one another from the first.

For some reason the radios scattered around the house seemed important to me when I thought of Carrie as blind. One was in the baby's room on the dresser next to the bassinet, another on the coffee table next to the sofa in the living room, and the third sat in the corner devoted to kitchen purposes. This was the one I had often seen her adjusting beside her loom as she worked. Now it sat on the long pine table next to one of her yellow mixing bowls. I remember now with horror how I reached up in the living room to remove my rain hat, only to find I had already taken it off and mislaid it somewhere in her house. It was as if there were something in my hair. I can't say how many minutes I was walking around, quietly, so as not to wake the baby, admiring how beautifully Carrie had set up her house. Her sofa and chairs were new, the thickly upholstered kind with the squared off cushions and buttresses. If the baby cries—I said to myself—I will be allowed to go in and cuddle her; Carrie would never fault me for that.

So little time seemed to pass by my watch and yet, anxious to see her, I threw my coat over my head and went outside briefly to call her name. But there was only the sound of steady rain, of trees brushing up against one another—like the quiet shuffling of slippers overhead. I again came into the house and put wood into her potbelly stove. How nearly her fire had come to burning out! It was then that I knew that something had gone wrong.

Perhaps I finally saw a shadow—for I had turned the living room light on—or some people say you can feel the presence of an object before you actually look. That is what I have heard. I can only tell you that for a split second I imagined— do you know how you anticipate seeing, before you turn, what you will see? I expected an immense mobile or something that Carrie had made for her living room. It would have been very like her to do that. I don't know what it would have been—driftwood and shells, I suppose, things she had found and put together with colorful woven fabrics in a way that no one else might have done.

Have you ever looked at a thing that you know you have seen before, something that is so familiar and yet you cannot name it? Then you will know what I mean. Perhaps I felt like the deer I had nearly run down as it turned white in the lights of the car. There were two of them, swaying slightly as I moved, high in the dead air of the living room. Just off the railing from the second floor, they were slightly wrinkled, gone purple now. Above my head something very like ripe plums hung out of the hem of her blue-and-white flannel, flowered nightgown. Then I saw on them the arches, Carrie's feet gone black and blue.

T H E coroner was still there when I opened the oddly painted cigar box for the officers to see. I was trying not to cry because the policemen were made brusque by my tears. Perhaps it was their harshness in the face of my grief that caused me to rush on so uncharacteristically. My oldest sister and I had quarreled over just that color of gold when we were painting model cars and dolls. I blurted this irrelevance out hysterically as if it interested them, showing them the box. A real orchid on top of it had been dipped in gold model-car paint. Inside, the red scriptlike letters spelled out her name. And in the container the minuscule dead animals on their sides: the mother shrew—like a fetus itself, no more than four inches long—and the three infant-pink offspring, their ears barely formed, each part of a chain, each holding with its mouth to the tail in front as immature mammals do. I thanked God that she had not been able to see until I thought of her touching them, her slow discovery.

Since then I have read about this many times in the *Encyclopedia of Animals*. There is a color photograph of them making a string of themselves so that they will not be lost one from the other as they scurry along. The babies weigh no more, the book says, than a fraction of a gram; and the mother's hind foot is no longer than half an inch. I put out my finger but I could not bear to touch any one of them. I could not make out quite what the officers said, but it did not matter. They were not talking to me.

There are other details I cannot forget: how she was trussed up so that she would not make a mess, the words I saw over the shoulder of the chief officer as he filled out one part of his report. "Self-inflicted," it said. "Deviant death." I watched them coming to their conclusions pointing at the cathedral ceiling and the brief loft. They said she must have scaled the second story banister and tripped along it like a mountain goat in order to tie the rope and throw herself off. And the child. Perhaps that has had the most lingering effect. There was nothing but a pillow under the blanket that afternoon when I pulled it back. No one has ever been able to account for it.

Though much of those hours is obscured by the shock, I know that I yelled at the police officer. My voice came out: harsh and upset.

"That's quite right, ma'am," he said. "Suicide is the living end in these parts. It never does much work out right."

Perhaps it is a small episode when torn out of the cloth of a whole life, but it is something I have never been able to forget. I think day by day that something will dawn on me and the confusion will all drop away. Carrie, from among the dead, will explain. I have a new office these days: a large colorful place shining with fluorescent light that looks out over a small part of the city and onto the docks and the factories. From here you can actually see the clouds releasing their moisture. They say that if you are with the company long enough you will rise into one of the highest floors in the building, and from there, it is rumored, you can catch direct light. Many days I lean my cheek against the cool window and watch the water running along outside the glass only a fraction of an inch away. I speak less now than before; I laugh occasionally. I get by, I suppose, as the best of them.

And who can say that it would have been different somewhere else if I had left and somehow gone home as my sisters wanted me to do. Even now when one of them calls on the telephone, I find for a moment that I am my old self. It almost frightens me to get those calls. At the end when I have felt so thoroughly pleased, one of my sisters is sure to ask me when I will get ahold of myself and come home where I would have friends and conversation, where again I could have stimulating work. It terrifies me to hear the click after the long good-byes. And, do you know, Riley, I have begun to think seriously of it—though it is now too late to get back my old scholarship for graduate school. Very often I think of my friend Carrie when I hear the dial tone.

It's then that I remember for some reason, though I can't think what, how once, when I was a younger woman, even before I knew you, I sat at a basement bar in an inn with a friend from my college. We watched through the glass side of a swimming pool, in a window over the half lit bottles of sherry and grenadine, a woman unaware. She stood in the shallow part, raised up on her toes slightly, buoyed by the water. An effervescence glistened among the light hairs on her legs. Her wavy hands floated down in front of us then to attach them-selves to the upper edge of the bottom of her bikini pants. The right foot lowered itself like a fish onto the turquoise cement, and then: great bubbles, one by one, floated from the rear of her suit. One by one, they caught the shimmer of the lights. "Here, here!" my friend cried out. "Here's to that!"

Just this week I was studying that moment so long gone as I stared out onto the billowing gray afternoon of the city. That friend married a man and disappeared as so many friends from college did. And then, I was staring toward the bay and thinking of the way the other junior officers now rushed to-gether several times a day and then only with reluctance part-ed again. Far down below the building, a bright red, slightly scalloped circle bobbed very slowly among the darker mass. Then I was plunging into the elevator and then into the crowd on the street. I could not get to it quickly enough. I do not know what misfortune I expected, but she looked straight at me. She smiled with honest pleasure just as she was forced along the street among the rest who were trying to claim a seat for the journey out of the city. The umbrella quivered above her head at arm's length as she tried to lower it. She was call-ing out to me. But I could not catch her meaning, Riley. I found with disappointment too bitter for words that she too was gone.

You will want to know that this morning Julie came in from school—she is eight now, of course, and draws and paints like mad and loves animals just as much as before. She still brings home every stray she finds. Today she walked in with a box. It had the lid on it, little triangular holes where the butter knife or handle of the spoon had gone in and been twisted to get it out again. I can still hear the squeak of the cardboard when you pull it out—worse than a piece of chalk at a bad angle on the board when you've just begun to concentrate. Air holes for stray animals. I made them very much the same when I was a child. But Julie this morning holds it out—a white cardboard shirt box. Once it must have been yours.

So, this morning Julie opens up the box and says, "See—it has a broken wing." And there is a bat. All lightly furred—brown—a fruit bat, I guess. Not big.

"Mama," Julie says, tugging at my sleeve; and there is her hand with a slight ridge of peanut butter on the back like always from where she's been rummaging in the jar before dinner time. "Mommy—" The bat is little—that much is true. If it were any smaller, I would run screaming from the room. "It's all right, Mommy," Julie ways. "It won't fly. Mrs. Wilky says it has a broken wing. No one has to be afraid it might get in someone's hair."

"It's o.k., Jule—" I say, looking away from the ceiling corners where I can imagine that it might perch. I look down to see those dark eyes in the box—so small—rodent's eyes, or a shrew's, or an infant startled early in life. "What have we got that bats eat?" I say. I have not completely lost control of myself. Her fingers pick at my sleeve as they did when she was tiny. My eyes follow her little fingernails.

You should see her. She is feeling very adult. Her one front tooth presses her bottom lip, and then there is a space where the next one should be, and then: a smaller corner of one. Milk teeth. Already on their way out.

"Mrs. Wilky says you might not let me keep a bat. Mothers don't like to inhabit bats," she says proudly, thinking she has repeated word for word.

We look at the little vulnerable thing. The bones in its wings like veins in a pair of dark leaves. The head like something terrible I have seen. Or, as Julie says, "like a bat's," her shyest giggle beside me like a lot of bells—sweet bells.

That was earlier. Downstairs the bat is flying around the darkened dining room light. Across the hall, Julie has soothed herself into a sound sleep under the constant night of this place. Her cries echo still. "Melvin won't come down! Mommy! Mommy! How could you! You've scared Melvin away, Mommy—" And I am up in my room writing this down, trying to end this all on a hopeful note. As you used to say, what are we if we give up our hope? People say that it helps to write down your dreams; the magazines suggest it constantly. So I thought to myself—might it not work for the real thing? And so I ask you now, Riley, now that I understand about your knee—what, what happened to her? Why do I feel so paralyzed? Why does it take me so long to understand anything in this place?

$\approx$*In Recent History*

W E had been living in the islands just off the coast for some years when the matter of X.D. suddenly came and went. Though the sun is pleasant enough in spring and summer, our island is hardly tropical. Its rough hide is stony and fraught with gorse. It is a seasonal place. Small lakes dot the area, and along its edges rocky cliffs drop off steeply into a brilliant sea. Autumn does not strip the land completely. There are evergreens, low lying at the center of the island, that tower toward its edges as if the substance of the conifers had been spun out by centrifugal force. Perhaps the most peculiar thing was the presence of the island's predominant small animal. Not squirrels or chipmunks or iguanas, but rabbits had overpopulated the island as if set down by an all encompassing and hocketing wind. These were the rabbits of story books, not your western gray or dusty brown hares. These were the immense fluffy white and black spotted bunnies, brown, white, beige; and the insides of their long thick nappy ears were pink. It was as if everywhere the island had an innocence to it.

One day in June at Egg Lake, Will and I ran across X.D. unexpectedly. Every summer since we'd known him he had been completely occupied with hauling king crab off the coast. We had never seen him enticed by summer events. At the lake some friends had gathered to show off in their kayaks. And he was there, too, as an observer, standing off to one side, his yellow blond hair fallen slightly into one eye, his face ruddy and clear. His shoulders and arms were built up from his job. And his eyes were like new robin's eggs. The irises shone so blue that the whites of his eyes seemed blue, too.

Will and I lived in an A-framed house in the woods. It was a small cabin, and I had fallen for it immediately—with its rustic log walls and its airy interior with the large sleeping loft. We had a wood stove, too, that filled the atmosphere with warmth. And we had our own pond and a brief deck that inclined toward it where I often lay to nap in the late afternoon. But our pond was not Egg Lake, hardly the size for several kayaks to have a running start. We stood next to X.D. that day and watched the enthusiasts on the dock breaking in a new young man. Among them a woman in jeans and bright red flannel shirt delighted us with her brogue and her ready confidence.

"If you're so impertinent as to go taking a dive," she cajoled the nervous initiate already in his craft, "don't fight the turn. Whatever you're doing down there, don't turn mollycoddle on us. Remember your moves and don't fight your boat." Then she laughed. "Do one more thing for your old instructor, will you?"

"What's that?" the boy asked.

"Hold your breath."

With that everybody laughed, the one in the boat least, of course, though he made a good attempt.

"Remember," she said, "it's cold as your old Wisconsin, but it's not so dark, and your 'yak will be righting itself if you just swing around like you learned and hold onto your pants."

"How long does it take?" the boy asked. "In case I turn over—just in case, I mean?"

She smiled warmly at him then. "Not a worry's worth. Ten counts. You, for one, can hold your breath that long," she laughed. She knelt down on the dock and leaned out to pat him earnestly on the back. "I know that for fact. You're holding it so tight right now you've practically strangled it. Relax."

Everyone laughed then, including the boy, and he paddled onto the blue disk of water and set the shimmering reflections of the trees into motion. It was as if he had stirred them up from the bottom of the lake.

"Why, X.D.," I said when he turned to us. "I thought you had abandoned us as of last week. Has anything gone wrong?"

"No, no," he said, smiling very broadly. He had a habit of hanging his thumbs on the front pockets of his jeans, accentuating the hardy, solid look of his upper torso, the narrowness of his hips. "I've had a sudden impulse toward retirement—temporarily. I'm roosting on my savings this season, just for once."

He called across the strip of water then to the woman in the red flannel shirt. Her hair was full and brown. She had a slight mouth, but her eyes were bright as little green apples; they gave a real zest to her face. "Tell him again to keep his eyes open if he turns around," he called to her. "Tell him the water's o.k."

The woman smiled over at X.D. brilliantly, and it was clear they had met before. Her name was Lindsey, and she'd been in the States for five or six years, living in many parts. It was hard to live on the island without being noticed, perhaps impossible. She had come in May to work at one of the clothing shops for tourists and had already begun to look for a more permanent place. It was like that. The same had happened to us. Will and I had arranged for a two-week vacation during a summer break from college and then we were looking for jobs so that we might stay on the island for good.

"So maybe we'll be seeing you this summer after all. That's very good news," Will exclaimed. We enjoyed X.D.'s company that much. If X.D. and Lindsey had not been together for the first time recently, it was obvious that they would be soon. Such happinesses, however brief, pleased us both since we had come to such deep happiness ourselves.

"There you see him—" X.D. said. We looked over in time to watch wet brown hair like an otter's lifting up with the edge of the kayak. The boy was upright again. There were his eyes pinched tight as if drawn by little pursestrings into his face.

O N E evening not long after the kayak encounter, X.D. and Lindsey came for an evening to our house. How happy they seemed together, how natural. Neither seemed in competition with the other; there was none of the telltale mocking humor of a relationship doomed to fail. And there was the steady encounter of their bodies, one arm brushing the other's, the gentle hand laid on back or thigh.

We sat together on the deck looking off into the pond, sharing a pitcher of lemonade under a soft breeze in the pines. Lindsey had taken off her shoes and rolled up the cuffs of her pants. It was early June, yet there was already summer heat. She extended her leg and then she waved her foot just at the top of the water and a circle went out, as if her footprint had been a dragonfly, something that light.

"So Lindsey," I said, "how do you come to us? Where were you before you got the island bite and couldn't leave?"

"Ah," she said, "I've left behind an entire career of waitressing. And I miss it—not one bit."

"She came up from Oregon," X.D. volunteered as if he were responsible for this news. I almost expected from his tone to see him lean back in his chair. "Yes," X.D. said. "She was raised in Dublin."

"You can't say whiskers there," she laughed, "without everyone knowing it. According to my relatives, I've been married and run off thirty-six times."

Will lifted up his glass. "A toast to Number Thirty-seven. But tell me, Lindsey, is there any truth in it? Have you ever run off at all?"

She waved her foot and threw back her hair. "Only six or seven times I've been chased all the way to Galway and back by Neanderthals."

"Seriously now."

"Only once, actually," she said, and X.D. leaned forward

slightly in his chair. Will later said he thought he saw the hair stand up on X.D.'s ears. "I was shackled up once to the city clerk. He liked most especially to study figures. Any old figure but mine."

"I see, I see," X.D. said mostly to himself, and then to us, "Isn't that hard to believe?" He looked onto her slender form affectionately.

"I guess he must have cared about you after all, at least a little bit," I said. "He chased you down finally in Galway, you say?"

"Tubs to the whale," she exclaimed quite cheerfully. "I took refuge in the Church. What could I do? He had himself a gun. I came into a state of sanctuary on the tune that it was not my man at all but my man's friend who was chasing me down with a pistol. 'He's a venomous tufthunter,' I said, 'who is driving my husband and my own self mean. It's lucky if we don't the pair of us commit a mass suicide.' It was the most secure four hours of my life—hovered over like a fuzzy new chicken by nuns and priests. It wasn't long until the truth came around that it was my own husband trying to get his hairy paws onto my pristine self."

"Are you still married to him then?" Will asked gently, almost as if it was of no concern. He scratched thoughtfully along the light brown edge of his beard. I could not help but admire Will. We had been together so long and yet he always seemed handsome and kind and new.

"Oh, no," she said gayly. "The Queen has seen fit to sever our hands. I was lucky enough to have married an infertile man."

Beside her X.D. smiled, and then tenderly he pressed her fingertips. The evening passed lazily and to our delight the two proved themselves to be compatible in conversation as well as in dreams.

THE following week I was visiting my friend Lisa in her trailer. She had the piece of land next to ours. Her place was a

fifteen-minute walk through woods and then there was a
clearing of quite high grass and in the center of it sat her trailer.
Once I likened her field to a veld and she pointed with her
good arm toward the horizon and imagined for both of us a
rhinocerous grazing, its tulip ears twirling away flies. The inside of her trailer was hung with tapestries and Peruvian
weavings that took away that trailer feeling, nearly completely, of being inside a tin can.

Lisa's right arm had been withered from birth but it had not
affected her sunny nature nor her attempts at pleasure in life.
She was small with brown hair drawn back into a swinging
braid down her back. She had a bad foot, as well; especially the
toes were affected. I saw them once when I arrived unan-
nounced. They looked as though they had been bound at
birth. I told her that and it gave her great satisfaction to think
she might have been made that way—in an earlier life, so she
said. That was the way she thought of things.

To support her fascination with the island, Lisa had taken
up cleaning house for the wealthy summer residents. On this
particular day there had been an alteration in her usual sched-
ule. She was to go to a new customer's house, she said, and
continue her preparations for their arrival at the end of the
month. She had been there only once, but she was certain I
would find it interesting if I wanted to go along.

We set off across the field along the footpath she and her
friends had beaten to and from her place. Before me, tilting as
she limped, her full black skirt swayed about her calves. The
bodice of the dress was also black and she seemed a shadow in
the grass when the sun cut through between the trees and
caught me in the face. She always wore a dress, she said, when
she went off to clean, because it made her feel unlike a true
servant in these times. She thought herself more of a character
in a book. She always wore one of three or four identical black
shirtwaists, and over it a crisp white pinafore. She had also a
white triangle with a violet embroidered on it to tie around her
braided hair.

The house was set on a point of land jutting into the water. The land did not fall off steeply as it did on most of the island but gradually and by way of a dock that casually stretched out. Soon there would come the summer boats and guests, the people to stand, drinks in hand, and bathe in the dry northern light before retiring to the city for three seasons again. Lisa was considering moving in to keep up the house in the winter, she said.

I looked up at the size of it. Above the gables and unpainted victorian scallops of the rooms were the many chimneys that would again descend to provide some heat to what I assumed would be large drafty rooms. We had not yet been inside. She had first to show me the small dark huts set about the land where the migrant workers had stayed—how many years ago?—to gather the tart cherries from the summer trees.

I only saw the house that once; but it is the sunroom I remember best: the immense porch with its untuned grand piano, the library adjacent and the worn wooden floor, the tables and their tatted cotton cloths, the brown wicker chairs. It was there I thought I saw them dancing; Lindsey and X.D. floating in the sunlight from off the ocean, both in tight new jeans, their faces glowing with relief.

X. D. had been seeing Lindsey for three weeks when we saw him again. How distraught he was when I opened the door. "Why, what is it?, X." I asked. "Have you got the summer flu?"

"No no," he said, but his voice was agitated.

"Sit down," I said. "I'll make you some tea or a drink. Will is going to be sorry to have missed you."

X.D. was a tea drinker, a habit he had picked up on some one of his travels he said. We had finished off many pots together, an insignificant fact anywhere else where imported goods were easily got.

In the living room, a roundabout story ensued. I could not

make out what the problem was even when X.D. said he'd stated it. He sat in the stuffed chair by the window, his elbows on his knees and his head forward as he stared at his hands. Lindsey, it seemed, wanted to go to the Fourth of July celebration. It was a tradition on the island and everyone would attend. Lindsey, with her enthusiasm, would not have missed such an event.

"I refuse," X.D. exclaimed to me. "I refuse to go to such a ludicrous charade."

"Why not, for heaven's sake?" I tipped up the teapot in front of him, and he watched the clear green liquid from the orient slip out into the cups. "How do you mean ludicrous?" I asked.

From a pontoon in the middle of Egg Lake at the center of the island, the rockets were shot into the sky. For the event the islanders separated themselves from the tourists by congregating on the mayor's private property around the narrow end of the egg.

X.D. scowled into his cup. "I can't stomach it—to applause!—the imitation of bombs. Lindsey thinks I'm berserk."

I laughed, wrongly perhaps, and tapped his arm. "I think you're partly berserk all the time." I smiled very briefly—until I caught the coldness in his eyes. "I'm sorry," I said. "I'd only occasionally thought of it like that."

"It's hideous, it's inhuman," he declared.

I looked at him in such surprise. He had never once seemed dauntable before. "I guess you're quite upset," I said. I could only think of one possible reason for it; but surely we would have known by then. He stared up from his cup, and I pushed him again. "You don't usually look quite so *hangdog*, X., not even when you're breaking up with your latest love. Tell me what's the matter, please. Maybe it will help. You're not already tired of her?"

He said nothing, just stared at me and then his hands. Quietly he was working his jaw. If he'd been asleep he'd have been grinding his teeth.

"So my sister sent me a book for you," I said, giving him

time to come around to telling me, if he wanted it that way. "It's the new biography of Freud."

The bookstore on the island was almost completely useless, and the local theatre brought in only children's movies. We were gluttons for imported culture, Will and I, X.D. too. X.D., who was particularly fascinated by Freud, barely raised his brow even at this news. How many times recently had he mentioned his anxiousness for the book? He said nothing, merely gazed at his own hands, hanging his blond head.

Finally I blurted it out: "After all this time, you're telling me you were in the war, X.D.?" It seemed almost as if he'd already said it anyway. "Is that what you're saying? All this time and all these talks and you've never before mentioned it?"

He looked up because he, of course, had not said any such thing that afternoon. "Yes yes," he said. "I don't like to talk about it."

"I can't believe you never even mentioned it."

He looked at me a long time then, and the blue of his eyes seemed almost heartbreaking in his suddenly worried lean face.

"All right, I was in Cambodia," he said. "The government said we weren't there. I trained mercenaries."

"Mercenaries? I didn't know there were any—"

"Yes," he frowned. "I was an officer, a captain. Yes," he said again, "in the Green Berets." His face had taken on a hardened, white look, as if he were concentrating very hard, or as if he were made of wax beneath the yellow stalks of his hair.

"Oh," I said, startled, for Will and I had been part of the resistance to the war. As X.D. knew, Will had for a time been in jail. "The Green Berets."

He shrugged as I looked on for the first time perhaps, in a quite different way, at his powerful arms. "I got in before anyone knew we had a right not to go. It was early. I'd like to think I wouldn't have gone if it had been later." He told me then one story after another, as though he had no way of stopping himself.

The recollection he seemed most to want me to hear was the one he introduced lightly at first. Adrenaline and the love of a friend, he said, could make a man of one hundred and eighty pounds carry another twenty pounds heavier for miles through brush and fire. It was the episode that upset him the most.

"Yes," he snarled. He leaned over and the glossy male face on the magazine seemed to stare up at him through his empty cup. He had broad shoulders and hands and a construction worker's rather short forearms. His hands and wrists were covered with fine hairs that caught the light as it infiltrated the room. His eyes seemed to tighten with intensity. "You know the incredible heat you feel when another human being is up against you, the satisfaction of it? I felt my own friend cooling against me. He was my warmth and then slowly he was my relief—from the jungle heat, don't you see?" He sighed then and stared at me harshly, almost proudly, as though I would never understand. "I think of that when I make love to anyone for any length of time."

"Is it the celebration itself worrying you? Or have you gotten too close to Lindsey now?" I asked. "Or is it both?"

His brow furrowed. "You have beautiful hair," he said. "Do you know that? It's like honey—the deep brown golden kind—made from alfalfa or something like that."

The sun was shifting through the trees behind him. Briefly he was a silhouette, his hair golden around his darkened face. I opened the tin of cookies on the table for him. "Tell me, X.D. You're driving us both crazy trying to get started. Jump in, I'm listening."

And so he did begin again, suddenly, looking me straight in the eyes. "I was sent to the mountains to train the Montagnards."

"As mercenaries, you said."

"Yes," he said. "A few of our men had been there before me as officers, but of lower rank. I was lucky to have one still there as an advisor—when I wanted him. And when I needed it. I hadn't been there long enough to have laid out my gear when the chief of the Montagnards invited me to his tent." As if to veer from the topic his worried eyes went toward the kitchen door. "I won't concern you with the menus of foreign lands."

"Would you like something else, X.?" I asked. "You've had lunch?"

"Yes, no thank you," he smiled. We leaned together a little over the table between us, just slightly. The light revealed his face again, the crow's feet that never disappeared—happy or sad. He stroked his cup with the thumb of his other hand, cradled it with both, and drank down the remainder of his tea. His lips were drawn tight as if at a touch he might dissolve into tears or rage, it was hard to say which.

"I was still with the rotten translator they'd sent from training camp. The man was like a machine. He understood both cultures, but he would never let on when the two were coming to a head. A complete asshole, the man would sit back and watch the conflict begin. I think he enjoyed it. In any case, I was at a bad disadvantage with the Chief right away. I bungled along a little with the words I knew.

"Then when we finished eating, a young girl was brought into the tent by several older men. She was not quite sixteen, so the translator told me for the Chief. A lot was made of the fact that her face was very clean and clear. Yes, I agreed, she is very beautiful. She is slender like a willow, I said, smiling and nodding like a fool. The Chief took her hand and held it out to me. A human hand, it seemed absurd. 'No no,' I said. 'I can't.' I waved her away. The Chief was incensed, but I stood firm. 'No, I can't.' The translator did not even offer me a look. It was the lieutenant who jabbed me with his elbow, his first advice to me. He excused himself, in both languages, saying very politely that he had been called by nature. I, by the grace of God, had enough sense to say the same thing."

Outside, the lieutenant explained the situation to him. The young woman was the Chief's daughter. He would have to marry her. It was like something out of a fairy tale, X.D. said, you could already sense the upcoming tragic parts.

"So you were to marry a complete stranger right then and there?"

"For the company's security, to say nothing of the integrity of the girl herself. I was the new, although visiting, chief. That was how they looked at me.

"It was a long festival. I thought then, a little like Halloween. And we moved into my tent. At first I resented her. I've always hoarded my privacy. Most of the men had been there a year or more. They would have given anything to have had her."

"She was that beautiful—"

"She was a woman," he said. "Beautiful, yes. The other women in the village were not free to consort."

"You were with her for a long time?"

"Two years. I was very gentle with Pom. I may have killed strangers," he said, "but I was very gentle with her." He looked me straight in the eyes. "I left her there. I suppose you'll say I've been leaving others ever since because of her."

"Why did you leave Pom then—if you loved her so much?"

"I was already married. My wife was waiting for me."

"Oh," I said quietly. Yet another fact about X.D. had come to light. "I see."

"My marriage was already finished, but I didn't find that out for certain until I got back. You can't tell that sort of thing from a distance. At least it was mutual. My wife and I just didn't either one seem to care anymore. And then one day almost a year later a friend wrote me that Pom was dead." He rubbed the fingers of his one hand with the other almost as if they were sore.

"I had made a string of gold coins into a necklace for her. We got so much money for each man we brought in dead. The money extended even to us. The necklace was supposed to be her legacy, I said, if I should get myself killed. She wore them constantly. She was superstitious about things. They wouldn't have had to kill her for them. She was very shy. She would never have stood up for herself. Even for me she would have been much too afraid."

He put his hands over both of mine for a moment and I

moved closer to him. Then he was holding my hands in his tight fists on his knee. "I'm sorry," I said.

"Yes," he said. "Yes, of course."

We were silent for a long time, suspended over our own reflections in the glass table. "And now there is Lindsey," I said. "She would understand, X.D. I'm sure she would. If she didn't, you wouldn't want her anyway."

"No," he said. "It's none of her business. If I thought you would mention it to her—"

"You wouldn't have to tell her the whole story, you wouldn't even have to mention Pom. The war is enough."

"That isn't why I told you."

"Of course not," I said. "I didn't think it was. All the same I could help you by talking to her. I could, or Will— It's obvious how much she means to you. You've made that clear to me."

"No." He was adamant. "A friend could not help me."

"You want her to trust you without explanation. Is that it?"

"I don't give a damn about trust," he scowled. "I want her respect."

Dr. Principal was known for a character on the island. He was nearing sixty, tall and wiry, with the same steel-rimmed glasses that he'd had for thirty years, so people said. He always wore short sleeves. It was almost as if he had on wings they stuck out so around his bony arms. He and I had become close friends. I had his confidence enough to hear many of the stories of his work that he would not tell anyone else. In this way I knew that he was very excited about the skull that was found on the island that summer. Roundabout town he had taken on the appearance of the nonchalant.

It was not everyday that he got to see a head without a body, he laughed. It was often enough, he said, that he saw them without brains wandering around town looking for the new sweet shop. He was adamant about sweets. Bold Expectations, he was certain, was destroying everybody's metabolism and sense.

No, he told me, the skull was not the head of the young

woman in the rumor I'd heard flying around. That woman had disappeared several years before Will and I had arrived. Dr. Principal himself had helped her to escape her more than tyrannical parents—although he could not publicly say such a thing. He knew her whereabouts still. No, he said to those who became concerned, there was no sense in worrying about that. The head was old, he said, very old, he knew that much.

Fourth of July week the island was intoxicated with the thought of it; the mayor sent for the expert on bones who was set up with a good room and a telephone in the East Island Inn. Even Will and I heard the buzz that went up among the young unattached women: the young archaeologist was a handsome sort. In any case, Dr. Principal said, he determined that the head was old, quite old, almost Neanderthal. Yes, a real cause for celebration on the island: a history that went beyond memory, right there underfoot. Who knew what else had happened on these very grounds? "Headhunters, that's what happened," Dr. Principal said to thrill the populace. "I'd bet my car on it." His hard-driven imported stationwagon was the only emergency vehicle on the island, except for a plane.

T H E next time I saw Lindsey was the second of July. She was brewing up a very large fret about X.D.'s refusal to go with her to the celebration. Her insistence was almost childish, I thought; but then I knew the reason behind X.D.'s seeming rejection of her, and I knew that he had said finally of Lindsey Byrne what he had not said of anyone else, that in her he had finally found someone he could both love and trust, the only one since Pom. The images of his experience had been lingering with me all week—how he had carried his friend like a child through the brush, whispering only to himself, "There there, there there."

Lindsey had decided upon several possible reasons for his sudden hardness toward her. She had settled too easily on the idea that it was another woman—either he did not want to be

seen with Lindsey at such a public event or he was going elsewhere with somebody else.

In the back of Bold Expectations she was telling her side of it
to Molly McAlester when I came up their alley, taking the
short cut to the post office. Molly was cleaning up the malted
milk containers and ice cream scoops when Lindsey caught
sight of me. Abruptly they leaned out the back door and
flagged me down.

X.D. had made me promise not to let on even to Will what
he'd said. It was too hard, he said, having other people know
about it. They changed their views, he said. They treated you
with pity if they knew you'd had pain.

I had tried to tell X.D. obvious things—that everybody had
tragedy. But he said everybody may have had it but everybody
didn't tell it.

"Yes yes," I'd said, mimicking him, after an hour and a half
of reasoning. "The things you staunch people won't do to save
face." With that we had come to a sudden and frosty halt.

Predictably, Lindsey was puzzled by the continued glum
view he had taken of the upcoming festive event. "I don't care
a rap about the fireworks," she said to me and to Molly. "I
want to know why the sudden change in his amorous weather, that's what."

Quickly I slipped out of the sweet shop, making a lame excuse. I have always been bound by my promises. All I said,
and even that was perhaps too much, was that X.D. never did
anything without a good reason and why not leave it at that?

As I turned to go, I saw in Lindsey's face a new determina-
tion. It seemed she and X.D. had talked intimately about
many other things. This reversal in his character had frightened her. He had come to mean a great deal to her in such a
short time, but she was looking out for herself.

J A M I E Hamilton was one of the better-liked young men on
the island, who had taken his unassuming position as post-
master the year after he graduated from one of the more prom-

inent law schools in the East. Though he had stayed near the head of his class, he soon found that he had no ambition. It was talking to people he preferred, not arguing their stories. His sudden lack of interest in the subjects he had studied was actually held in his favor by the more reclusive native islanders. It was said that the most important thing Jamie had learned in law school was to juggle fruit. Standing in a second floor apartment or office, gazing serenely out one window or another, it was not uncommon to see suddenly three or four, maybe even six, objects whirl up from below. There was no reason to look down. There would be the red hair of the eldest of Mayor Hamilton's remaining red-haired boys, his lean arms a comic blur. Jamie's older brother had not come home from the war. Perhaps this was partially why people approved of Jamie's return even from the profession of his choice.

Now it seemed to everyone as if he had never once been away. "Coming out to Egg Lake for the festivities this year?" Jamie called out when he saw me at the counter. Something about Jamie always reminded me of a young strutting rooster. He was a good looking man with his reddish hair, the long jaw, and very quick way of moving. This year, as in every recent year, Jamie was to be in charge of the fireworks display.

"Of course," I said. "I wouldn't miss your performance for anything."

His head cocked to one side, proudly. "I trained eight years for it. The first thing I learned in Boston was to shoot off my mouth, then I learned how to inflame the average crowd. Finally, I invented the incendiary comment." He didn't often talk about it seriously with people, I guessed. My sister had recently moved East. Perhaps that knowledge and the address on the package had reminded him again. He took out his circular stamp and pressed its red kisses all over the box. "You know," he said, suddenly sincere. "I was never much of a lawyer really; I was never anything but a gossip anyway."

"That's not what I hear," I said, examining the new postage stamp selections.

"Who's talking about me?" he laughed again, pushing forward the sheet of stamps with all the brightly colored birds posturing on the front.

"Why, the whole town is talking, talking about the darling of the harbor, of course."

"Ha," he laughed. If Jamie had been any younger you would still have seen his freckles. As it was you only imagined you saw what had recently gone. "Free legal consultations have earned me a few points."

"It's a miracle you don't go hungry you've got so much giveaway business," I said. "So what's new around and about?"

"Have you heard about Dr. Principal's latest patient? The doctor's got a human head in his vault over at the office."

"A human head," I scoffed as if I hadn't heard. "Why, Jamie, now you've gone too far."

"Honest to God," he said, rocking the hand-canceling device over the letters he had taken from one of the canvas bags hung up on the wall. "Tourists found it down along Whipple Road. Authorities are trying to put a trace on it."

"But in his vault, Jamie—won't it make a horrible stench?"

"The vault's in the refrigerator where he keeps all his specimens. Took out a few of the racks, I guess. 'Jamie,' Doctor said to me yesterday, 'I never dreamed when I bought the vault I was buying a kind of a hat for a head completely unattached in the world. And now the specimen fridge has turned into a hatbox on me, too. Next thing you know they'll say I'm mad as a hatter myself.'

" 'Dr. P.,' I said, 'The next thing you know is already behind you. Better turn around.' "

THREE-QUARTERS of the year, ferries ran only once a day. I loved the isolation of that, particularly in winter. Will and I and some friends had taken up filling in the long winter evenings with writing letters on behalf of imprisoned civil rights activists around the world. We had had some success. In the beginning we had been doubtful that such a small group of us could have an effect, but then there were many groups like us scattered about. But in the summer the nature of the island took on quite another aspect for us. There were thousands of tourists, and the boats came every other hour. The cars streamed off like ants. People came wheeling their bicycles down the ramps with their dogs at their heels. Children in groups swarmed after lone beleaguered adults.

Year around, I worked in the small insurance building across the street from Dr. Principal's office. In summer, we often had our sack lunches together, sitting on the big rocks overlooking the small blue port stuck with masts and fishing boats and nets. The little cream-colored restaurant sat below. There the clam chowder was good in late autumn and winter. There no islander would enter during the summer months, it was so besieged.

Each year the Fourth of July was particularly rough on Dr. Principal since he was the only doctor on the island. He had made a new partnership with two other doctors but they were not to arrive until the beginning of the year. Each summer the doctor expected numbers of broken limbs and, the way the tourists took the small winding dirt roads of the islands at full speed, perhaps even an automobile accident. An entire family had been lost the year before I came, Dr. Principal said. They'd been so lost that he'd not even seen a body of them until the auto floated up and headed, upside down, into shore at Sheepshead Bay. There it gave a group of holiday bird watchers a terrible start. The Doctor had been napping after work each day for two weeks, in preparation for the coming weekend's events. Fifteen minutes only, he said, that was all he could give himself, but still he could feel it accumulating under his skin.

There was a joke that Dr. P. was the worst automobile driver around. In all the taverns on the island a jar sat on the bar for the collection of contributions to buy him a siren for his car. It was a small imported station wagon that flew as if it had no speed control at all, no driver at the wheel. Down the winding roads the vague beige vehicle tore in a ghostlike dust. Dr. Principal himself encouraged this modern headless horseman image, in hopes that both the island natives and their visitors might drive with vigilance.

Thus it had been rumored, a sort of unintended repercussion of his self-perpetuated story, that Dr. Principal was a mediocre airplane pilot—a truly unjust charge. He was the only doctor not only on our island but on the other three that made up the chain. If a case was really serious, Dr. Principal carried the wounded to the mainland hospital himself in his own Piper Cub. He had never had a scrape.

At Dr. Principal's urging I was thinking of taking flying lessons. Neither of the nurses in his clinic had wished to be on relentless call as he had, and they as a pair had made it clear that they refused to fly. I would manage the plane, and Dr. P. would be free to watch vital signs and see to the patients while in the air.

As it was, he was confined to piloting for a good twenty minutes of crucial lifesaving time. Whenever I woke from sleep, I thought of him and considered his plan. I almost believed I could hear the whining of the plane overhead—though that would have been impossible. The tiny cleared field that served as his runway was on the other side of the island—at least fifteen miles away from where we lived on Egg Lake. Dr. Principal frequently reminded me: We would be good together, he and I. A team.

I T was Will's birthday the day before the Fourth and X.D. was at our piano pounding out songs of celebration. *My friend Will,* X.D. sang half in jest, as if from me, since I could not play. The piano had come with the house. I carried in the cake and the three of us celebrated Will's birthday together. At the last moment, in an argument, Lindsey had decided not to come along with him.

That night X.D. again alluded to his love for Lindsey. I remember because Will repeated what he'd said later after he had gone. He and Lindsay were like cougars together, X.D. said, like absolute cougars. He had never experienced anything like it. When I heard it the second time, I thought quietly to myself how much he must have loved the lieutenant, his good friend, whom he had carried desperately through the jungle because the boy had had both of his legs blown off above the knees.

"D o we see you tomorrow at the celebration?" Will asked as we walked him to the door. We always had a small dinner of our own at home, perhaps inviting one or two people to join us before going off to the fireworks which were practically next door at Egg Lake. X.D. glanced at me for a moment but I said nothing.

"You and Lindsey could come over before the fireworks in any case," I said. "No matter what you do later."

"But why wouldn't they go to the fireworks," Will said as if there was no question of it. "You *must* go to the fireworks— since you're going to be around this year. It's the best display anywhere. There's something practically Chinese—ancient Chinese—about it. Not the usual popcorn display. Well, you'll see."

X.D. was looking out over the pond, his jacket over his arm. The nightbirds had already begun to fly, and I heard an owl and then a nighthawk and the scamper of creatures in the underbrush. "I guess," X.D. said.

I smiled wanly from the doorway as he drove off. I had come increasingly to resent and pity him for putting me into such a predicament.

The next day we had no rain. Rain had been threatened by the mainland weather stations, but the islanders had scoffed. There had never been foul weather on the Fourth in the history of the island as far as anyone could recall. Even in the extended memory of the older and more lucid nursing home patients, no one could report it. I went about gathering things for our supper, enough for four if Lindsey and X.D. should show up. If not, I had no objection to eating leftovers the following day. There were good scallions and tomatoes at the store for our annual potato salad, and I laid in several bottles of wine. Out back there was a layer of rock with mosses and wild strawberries flung over it as if someone had decorated a hat. For dessert we would have strawberries and cake. And we would grill a chicken or two over a maple-leaf charcoal fire.

Often we spent this part of the evening alone together, Will and I. Will in the end was the only one surprised when X.D. and Lindsey did not arrive; I was more than a little relieved. Perhaps they had stayed elsewhere on the island to be together quietly, I hoped.

Cars were lined up along the road from Egg Lake as far as we could see as we walked in across the field. On the door of Lisa's silver trailer were strung across the screen perhaps fifty small American flags. The moon was already on the rise, a great red strawberry moon hanging as if by a string in the trees, and beneath it: a stag and a faun were caught in evening light. Will and I stood looking in turn at them through the binoculars. Lately we had a growing concern for the very young, it seemed. Only within the last few months had we begun to consider aloud the possibility of having a child. I gave Will's beard a tug when the doe moved into sight, and he handed the glasses back to me. How completely silky the faun's spots seemed, how lopsided on its quivering young back.

In recent years we had taken to watching the fireworks from the hill. There we were elevated above all the people, yet the display would rise high over us. With the help of the glasses, we could see below in the waning daylight the tourists seated in a vast crowd in the meadow. The much smaller group of islanders gathered near the west end of Egg Lake on the private property of Mayor Hamilton. The only cars in sight now were those of Dr. Principal, Sheriff Watts, and the Hamiltons. The rest had been left back on the road.

Perhaps ten or twelve of the island's young men were on the pontoon in the middle of Egg Lake which served as a natural barrier to the curiosity of the crowds. There was Jamie Hamilton with his fellows from the Chamber of Commerce making their preparations on the platform. Dr. Principal and his wife were seated on a blue and red plaid blanket with a large picnic basket. "Look, Dr. Principal made it out of the office," I said, and then I sighed a little sadly and handed Will the glasses. "He's having one of Lisa's chocolate pies."

Will looked down across the clearing. It was the doctor's custom to barter his services to people from the island who couldn't pay. "Don't worry," Will said. "Maybe it's just good will. A friendly gesture. Lisa's been known to do that."

"Yes, that's true," I replied, unconvinced. It was bad enough to be ill without also being broke.

"Lisa looks all right," Will said. "Same as ever. And there's the doctor's usual centerpiece.

Dr. Principal carried his walky talky with him at all times. He received his messages through the sheriff's office, squawking and barely discernible. "Here it comes—" Dr. P. often said to me when the thing went off, "the call of the wild."

We had brought with us two bottles of bug repellent, one in case the other was lost. I was working on Will's back now. First a kiss, then a neck massage and then a cover up of mosquito sauce.

"Don't forget my ears."

"I wouldn't," I said. "What costume's Lisa got on?"

"The usual."

"Hmm," I said. "No embellishments? Not a hat this year? Or a crown?"

"No."

I didn't have to look, though it always amused me to see it. She would be wearing her red, white, and blue ankle-length dress with the one bared shoulder and the immense star over the right breast. Her hair would be let loose from its usual braid to stream wildly about her shoulders; and on her feet were surely the sparklingly red, metallic orthopedic shoes.

"Now I'll do you," Will said, and we exchanged the field glasses for the insect repellent.

I had been surprised to find at our first experience of the island's celebration that there was no music. Nearly fifteen years before, musical instruments had been outlawed indefi-

nitely by the town meeting. A hard-rock version of the national anthem, tried out by the high school band during one
year's grand finale, had been the cause.

The fireflies in the dusk of the meadow below made the field
seem vast. And then I saw, in the circles of the binoculors,
X.D. and Lindsey on the other side of the egg with the rest of
the islanders. There was X.D. sitting close to Lindsey on a blue
and red blanket, just like the doctor's, as the sun went down.
Lindsey's head was tilted up at X.D. On the pontoon the rockets were lined up along the edges on small posts and there
hung all their ropelike fuses. Under our own blanket on the
cliff, Will and I would soon be snuggled up together so near
and yet so far away from them. "Will—" I said. "There are
X.D. and Lindsey."

"Good," he said, but then his head turned up toward me.
"What's the matter? Isn't that a good thing?" Will had just
finished oiling my ankles and patting the lotion onto the back
of my blouse.

"I promised X.D. I wouldn't tell anyone," I blurted out, "not
even you. But something might happen tonight. I don't want
to be the only one knowing—" Already I felt ashamed for
breaking my word.

And so we sat on the cliff and while I told Will all that X.D.
had said to me, we watched X.D. stroke the side of Lindsey's
face and hair. "No," Will kept saying as I went along, "are you
sure?" When I came to the end, we looked down at them together kissing on the blanket in the sunset. Will said, "He told
me he was a peace activist during the war."

"He never mentioned it at all to me," I said, incredulous. "I
just assumed it, I guess, from all his other talk."

"He even described several marches," Will said. "I remember it clearly. He was arrested, he said. So! he actually felt
he had to cover up."

"Why on earth do you think he came tonight." It was not a
question. We exchanged the glasses. Far below on the other
side of the tip of the egg, their figures seemed mere cutouts,
like those of a courtly couple set against a pastel country

scene, the kind one sometimes saw in old picture frames. Our friends were staring at one another, talking with very little gesture, completely rapt.

Down below I could see with increasing difficulty the children playing leapfrog at the edge of the woods. Dogs nosed in zigzag fashions along the ground. The people from the nursing home huddled in their lawn chairs, light summer blankets over their laps. Couples everywhere were pressing hands, their thighs close on the grass. And then I could not see any of them. The lake, too, had been obliterated, and with it the pontoon. The sky was all there was.

The initial blast was a loud cracking white starburst and then others whistled out on tendrils, small, carnationlike, in every direction in pink and white and blue. One by one, the missiles catapulted with violent and exhilarating sound into the air, there to explode light and airy as dahlias, like Chinese flowers.

In the dark I felt for Will's hand. It was also the pontoon we were watching, the closest thing to being able to see X.D. who, we knew, would be watching anxiously. First there was the slight glow of the torch and then the arched and leaping brevity of light that was the fuse, and then a high-pitched whistling streak of broader flame as the projectile shot into the air followed by the concussive force above, of air bursting against air. For nearly an hour we looked on at the white and blues, the reds and greens and yellows, the silver and gold. Perhaps the only reason that both Will and I were watching when the rocket misfired was our concern for the way X.D. was seeing things from that blanket on the ground.

There was no whistling of the ascent, only the explosion and a cry of a human or animal in pain, and then the communal gasp of friends and strangers alike across the whole field. Something was burning and screaming on the deck of the boat itself. Almost simultaneously the shouts of young men started up and then a spark on shore as the flashlight of Dr. Principal showed up the lower half of his own face as he grabbed up his medical bag. We saw the shaft of light aim toward the boat. Then there on the shore X.D.'s form was running toward it, too. I saw his body lift up and then his shallow dive. It was maybe fifty yards to the pontoon. Whatever had been burning on deck was no longer on fire. Jack Watts was speaking through his bullhorn in a monotone advising the tourists to stay exactly where they were. We could see almost nothing at all now, as the crowd moved in and we headed down the steep slope along the circuitous long path, moving toward our friends who seemed now so far away in the light of the moon.

On shore Mayor Hamilton had trained the lights of his own car on the boat and was turning on the doctor's, too, when it all came into view. On the deck in the sudden light lay one of the mayor's red-haired sons. And there Dr. P. stood at the edge of the water waiting as the pontoon started to move its heavy cargo toward the shore. We could not see whether or not X.D. had been pulled aboard. We could hear the heavy churning of water and then the young men were going ashore. Dr. Principal was leaning over someone and then he was running toward the lights of his wagon on the dirt road. To our astonishment the station wagon was speeding out of its reserved place on the lot; the Hamilton boy had been left exactly where he lay. Mayor Hamilton and the rest of his family bent over him and there, too, was X.D. beside them in the lights from the car. It was as if they were on stage, but we could not see which of the Hamiltons was on the ground until X.D. moved to put his arm around the mayor's wife. "Oh no," I said. But Will had already gripped my arm.

Jamie's features were caught and glowing along with X.D.'s blond hair like two spots of warmth in the dark. As we hurried across the meadow around the top of Egg Lake, we heard Lindsey calling to Lisa. The sheriff's voice rose again, loud and hollow, explaining the accident only in general terms at first. The people in the crowd were to drive their cars in single file, he said, along the sides of the meadow and park with their headlights on low beam. When we crossed the opposite corner of the field, we could see in the row of car lights Lisa's wild hair and flowing gown, where she was directing the traffic with her flashlight.

As the rest of the crowd hurried to clear the field, to make the path of light, Will and I reached the boat quite easily. Already the sound of an airplane engine droned increasingly overhead. The field was nearly vacant now, and the long row of lights crept steadily along the borders of the woods. The rectangle was nearly complete. It was as if torchbearers had gathered to hold a silent vigil there. The last pedestrians disappeared then and we stared for a second at the meadow that had been emptied so quickly. We had been too far away, come too late to have been any help at all. The deputy sheriff asked us to stand back, and it was as if we were staring into an empty football field.

Overhead we could hear the Doctor coming in. One red and one green speck of light moved steadily against a field of stars. An immense shadow seemed to fill the sky over one end of the clearing, and then the plane dropped down in the dazzling aisle of light. It bounced along the open ground to halt not very far from the lake itself. And then I heard a sound I will never forget: Jamie—high-pitched, desperate, and quavering. Six people were hoisting Jamie in the blanket they had stretched among them; they were running across the field to the plane. Those who had not come in cars were hushed in a body up against the west shore. We heard a quiet purring of automobiles behind the sounds of grief-stricken cries.

We watched the plane lift up out of the broad sparkling runway, a shadow again, and then the lights of the plane grew small like fireflies, and then smaller still as they headed toward the the large red moon that hung over the mainland that night. In silence, we turned homeward, only to pass on our way the young kayak student, who had perhaps seen everything, crouched now, sick and coughing in the reeds. I wanted to stop, but the boy screamed at us more than once to leave him alone. Will pressed me against his side, and we went away.

A F T E R X.D. left the island, Dr. P. told me how our friend had claimed to have been a medic in the war. In that way Dr. Principal had decided to leave Jaimie and fetch the plane rather than take him over bumpy roads and fly from the airstrip. He also decided to take X.D. along rather than one of Jamie's relatives, or even some of the islanders trained in first aid. On the pontoon he had handed X.D. his own medical bag.

When they landed, the doctor had been heartbroken to find the bag untouched and X.D. unconscious in a state of shock, both of the young men's torsos soaked in blood. Cheek to cheek they lay, X.D. on top with his face hanging down over Jamie's shoulder, as if he had been whispering in Jamie's ear. Jamie's arms were tightly linked around X.D.'s arms and back. X.D.'s blond hair had been newly drenched in sweat. They could not tell at first, which had been the primary victim of the blast. The emergency room attendants had had to pry them apart. The missile fragments lay cradled between the two men in the hollow of Jamie's abdomen.

X.D. had never been a medic at all, Dr. Principal believed. Not even rudimentary attempts to stop any bleeding had been made. X.D. was treated and released the following day. It was said that X.D. refused to leave the hospital until Jamie Hamilton's family had come to carry his body away.

After that night X.D. withdrew from his usual activities. We saw very little of him before he moved. When he wasn't working on his boat, he stayed at home. He avoided Lindsey and just as thoroughly avoided us. For some reason it surprised me that he looked no different when I did see him. How strange and painful to see his face, as if he had not one secret terrible moment in his heart. How terrifying to watch him turn away down a street as if he had never lived there at all. Then, like so many from that war, he simply disappeared. One day he was there and the next no one could find him at all.

For a few of us the thought of him seemed slowly to subside, only to swell again and again along with the thought of Jamie Hamilton. Each year we sat quietly in reflection while the rest of the island glittered and rocked. Yet for most of the islanders, and even for the most unconsolable of us, time, which had seemed to stop, began again to move. Sadness and remorse gave way to living, growing things. Finally a catalog of changes would seem not to admit that anything had happened at all.

The tourists, as always, come gaily and go. Lisa became the new postmistress and in the summers wears some new costume each day. This year the mayor's third son went away to the same eastern law school Jamie once attended. And Lindsey, after worrisome grief and loss of weight, opened a scuba diving shop on the far end of the island with the man who became her husband, a handsome man, strong and bright. He is the second cousin of the archaeologist who came to investigate the skull Dr. Principal kept in his clinic refrigerator—as a talisman, he said. Here people have come to mark time by that. "That was the year the Doctor found the skull," people say. They have forgotten that he only examined it. Dr. P. finally convinced me to get my pilot's license. He helped me train; and now I work for him in his office as well as in the air. Soon I will be taking a six month's break, and a nurse will be coming over from the mainland while I am away. Any day now Will and I, under Dr. P.'s supervision, are expecting to deliver our new little Emily or Christopher.

In a broader sense there have been few incidents. Come autumn last year the usual epidemic of salmonella swept in on the heels of the annual red tide. This time the highest rate of infection occurred among the new technicians at the marine laboratory on the Point. Fortunately no lives were lost. No, it seemed they had never heard of such a thing, Dr. Principal said, though it happened nearly every year and it was their job to study similar things. The famous skull was moved to make way for all the specimens. And—though another year has passed, and it is once again berry time—the skull still sits on top of the filing cabinet beside the new receptionist's desk, where, as Dr. Principal says, people can take a long, hard look at it.

About the Author

MEREDITH STEINBACH was born in Story County, Iowa. She is the author of two novels, *Zara* and *Here Lies the Water*, and was a recipient of the Pushcart Prize and the 1990 O. Henry Award for her short fiction. She has been awarded fellowships and grants including those from the National Endowment for the Arts and the Bunting Institute of Radcliffe College, Harvard University. Her work has appeared regularly in *TriQuarterly*, and in other literary magazines including *Southwest Review, Massachusetts Review, Antaeus, Ploughshares, 13th Moon, Antioch Review, Tyuonyi*, and *Black Warrior Review*. A graduate of the Iowa Writer's Workshop, Ms. Steinbach has taught at Antioch College, Northwestern University, and the University of Washington. She is Associate Professor of English at Brown University. She has recently completed her third novel and is at work on her fourth.